I0571356

Enchanting
Agency

ND KALNA

Copyright © 2015 ND Kalna

All rights reserved.

This novel is entirely a work of fiction. The names, characters
and incidents portrayed in it are the work of the author's
imagination and not to be construed as real. Any resemblance to
actual persons, living or dead, events or localities, is entirely
coincidental.

Blue Pop Publishing

ISBN: 0692547886
ISBN-13: 978-0692547885

CHAPTER ONE

Let's take a "baseline" as the researchers say. When you have the chance, wear something nondescript, go someplace unfamiliar outside, find a place to sit down and wait. Wait for a person professionally dressed, or at least dressed nice, preferably of the same gender and slightly older than you. When you see them, do not make any judgments about the person.

"Wait a second," you say, that is, if you're paying strict attention, "you just said wait for a professionally dressed person. Is that not a judgment? Whether or not someone is dressed nice?"

Well fine, you're right, good pick up, but no more judgments and relax—act natural. Watch this person closely without any expression on your face. At some point they will *look* at you. Do not look away, do not smile, do not frown, remain expressionless and *look* right back at them. Observe. What you encountered is your "baseline." Remember your observations, opinions and thoughts about this person and, most importantly, this encounter because in the future when you try this observation experiment, you may experience horror.

This is confusing, so I am going to be straight with you.

It's a lot to grasp. I used to think history was boring, but now I have a new found respect because history sorts things out. The best place to begin is the history of Punishment, with a capital "P."

Did you know that people used to torture, maim, and kill others in the name of Justice, with a capital "J?" For example, during the American colonial era, if a woman gave a weird wink, maybe stared a little deranged at someone and that someone got sick, well then an investigation took place. The bearded investigators in sad-colored garments surround the house of the accused and maybe they find some bloody chicken feet in a stained wooden bowl sprinkled with supposedly noxious herbs from the adjacent dark woods. The accused woman goes on trial—a proper, patient, organized and earnest trial. Witnesses are called and cross-examined; rules of order and fairness are maintained. The jury of peers finds her guilty of witchcraft. The judge must choose from a plethora of punishments.

In most cases, the judge decides death by burning at the stake. Is there a cheer from the public? The witch, formerly just a woman, is tightly tied to a wood pole, her head bound rigidly against the splintering wood. Below her the people light a small fire, flickering at first, then, gradually, it grows in painful intensity. Eventually, after much screaming, a few hours later, she's turned to ash.

This was an awful time in history, but consider contemporary notions of justice. What is 'reforming' an individual if not a spell cast against them? Am I saying witches exist? Hmm, how about you be the judge? Or should I say, you be the researcher?

CHAPTER TWO

I didn't come up with these ideas in an afternoon, you know. These thoughts had long been incubating in the inferno of my 'new' life in dumb-near-nowhere suburbia. My journal entries give insight into how my thinking evolved. I was a sophomore in high school in a new school and a new town at the time I wrote the following:

DATE: _____

I called the police, then my mother. Both are rushing to the house. Mom suggested I write down what happened to help me remember, get my thinking straight.

The first time I met the man chasing me was a few weeks ago at an interview with the Agency downtown. Bored, Mother on the phone, I left the waiting room to peek around, what an odd office. I witnessed some odd behavior. I almost stood close enough to see into a vibrating room, glowing blue. Glowing Blue! I definitely heard a person plotting to spread something.

The man could have been staring at me for a long time. He had brown hair and eyes, wore black or brown slacks, a white shirt, some tie, all covering an average height middle-aged body, gut slightly out. Once I noticed him, he quickly took three or four steps directly at me. I started to apologize, he simply ignored me, and continued right towards me. I had to jump out of his way. Did he want to stand in my place to see my view of the room? I couldn't see anything in truth, only a blank flat-screen TV failing to give even a ghost of a reflection. I got past him that day. He stayed in the blue glowing room. The color blue attracts children more than any other color.

Today the SAME middle-aged man came to my high school. I knew the Agency planned on removing all the soda. I couldn't get a close enough glimpse earlier, so I asked Ms. Mahner if I could go to the bathroom. Of course she said "no" and I gave her the old cramps excuse and a desperate expression. Once out of the classroom, I checked all the machines. The machines were going to stay, the soda was replaced with sealed juice and bottled water, great.

On my way to the last machine, I turned a corner and about 30 feet away a man crouched, a blue plastic soda bottle in hand, his head bowed, injecting a syringe into the bottle. He snapped his head up and looked into my eyes, instantly recognizing me. The next thing I knew I'm sprinting down the hall. Angrily he yelled "hey!" pursuing me with heavy slapping boots echoing off the walls in the hall. Thankfully, the bell rang and students poured out of the classrooms.

I had no place to run because I have no one to Trust. Ms. Mahner is not to be trusted; she drinks from sealed bottles. My new house seemed to be the only choice. Across the street and near Burger King, I peeked back at the school and the middle-aged man casually stood at the edge of the parking lot gazing over my peers' heads. I quickly ran into Burger King not knowing if he saw me or not. If I stayed outside and ran, he would have spotted me for sure.

All I found for safety was a booth, partially hidden from the front door if I laid flat on the seat. I could slide underneath the table and use the side door if needed. For a while nothing happened. No one even noticed me. Then there he was, he stood fighting for air. My cell phone went off. I dashed for the side door, and before I made it outside I heard a loud crash. Cutting into an alley, I followed a side street into my subdivision I thought my dad took before.

I kept running. I might not be able to run fast, but I can run for a long time. We moved here a month ago so I'm not familiar with all the roads. I got lost. All the homes in this suburb look the same. All the yards look the same. Although I remember shapes mowed into some of the lawns: a cake with candles, a happy face, two doves kissing, a dog sniffing the ground near a fire hydrant, etc...

No surprise about who called me, Michelle, my boss from the Agency. The man must have called her and she then called me so that he could capture me in the burger place. All of them must be aware about me now...

The police arrived so late in the evening that I had finished my journal entry and still had time to rock back and forth on the edge of my bed like a distressed mental patient. Mom still had not arrived and I already knew her excuse, "traffic." Someone banged on the front door. Alone in the house, I checked the peephole of the front door, and tried to stop jittering. The officers wore their reflective silver sunglasses despite the dismal lack of sunshine. I opened the door and they asked who I was. They wanted to talk to me outside. I couldn't trust them with everything; they could be one of them or under their control.

One of the officers asked me what happened. The other, behind his reflective glasses, silently glared at the house window in my general direction. I rambled.

"Slow down," he said.

I restarted with a description. After I finished he turned to his silent partner and remarked, "the only surveillance camera at that school faces the faculty parking lot. Maybe he got lunch near the school." Their postures were too rigid, their uniforms stiff.

The officer pointed his mirror-glasses back at me and told me to start from the beginning. Ha! The 'beginning,' that would be my first contact with the Agency. For these two potential spellbound men with guns, I decided to start at school and going to the bathroom. When I got to the syringe the police officer told me to repeat what I saw in the syringe.

He interrupted me, "wait, the color of the soda is blue, right?"

"So…"

"So he wasn't injecting the syringe, he was removing soda."

I tried not to appear stunned. Could it be, the man wasn't infected, he was studying the soda? Was some of the soda missing from the bottle? He certainly couldn't have injected more. He must have recognized me from the

Agency and chased me because he thought *I* was one of them.

"You were saying that he works for an agency?" The silent officer scanned the houses across the street.

"I haven't a clue. I hadn't seen him before."

An uncomfortable firmness gripped the officer's voice, "but you said you saw him before. Where?"

"Oh, at school before he chased me; I doubt he works with the soda truck. I mean, like I said, he wore a tie."

"I understand, he works for the soda company."

"Well, this is a new soda so maybe the company needed it back."

"Yes we know it's new."

They knew, of course they knew. My stomach felt loose inside me, as if it detached from the rest of my organs. I acted natural.

"So after you saw him, what happened?"

"He said 'Hey!' and I ran." I couldn't suppress a gulp any longer. Both officers tilted their heads down at me. "I could like hear him running after me and then the bell rang. I ran all the way home."

"The last bell of the day, for all the kids to go home?"

"Yes, *people* came out of the classes right away."

"Did he continue chasing you after the bell rang?"

"Well, I just ran, I can run for a really long time."

The silent officer took a step closer and, in a surprising normal voice, asked, "do you," he paused, "want to add anything else," and he forced a cynical smile.

He wanted the gesture, the wink, the word. I could only stare up at them, their humanity hidden behind silvery sunglasses. They waited.

A vicious plastic scraping sound broke the standoff; my mom had scraped the bumper speeding into the sloped driveway. The officers took a few steps back as my mom approached me.

"Oh my God honey! Are you alright?"

"I am now."

"Thank you for coming officers."

"No problem ma'am, we've finished getting all the information from your daughter. We don't believe the man specifically targeted your daughter, she should be fine. We'll go to the school now unless you need anything else. And please do not hesitate to call us."

"Thank you so much. Honey let's go inside, and tell me what happened." During the exchange, somehow, someway, my mom had given them the sign, the wink, the gesture to let them know she is one of them.

• • •

You know what? This is too much to jump into: businessmen chasing me at my high school, spellbound police officers, even my mother as a receipt of the virus and giving coded gestures. It's simply too much. Why did I go from viruses to witches? Well, like a said, history helps.

My introduction to the virus started with the Agency, but the real story starts with my family's move to a new suburb of a new city. We drove to the new home. I lost myself in thought for the whole trip staring out a dripping window listening to the singular sound of tires on a wet rainy highway. At this point in my life, staring at the dripping window, if I could do the observation experiment, i.e. look at a stranger, "baseline," I would think, well, possibly a lot of things. One thing I would not think is that the stranger threatened my existence.

From the driver's seat my father slightly lifted his head, "just think Eleanor, you can *start completely anew* at your new school." Peering at me through dark-ringed eyes in the driver's mirror he added, "you can reinvent yourself." His sleep deprived eyes tried to smile.

Every muscle had gone tight in my body and I succeeded in checking a scream—Reinvent! My knuckles turned sheet-white gripping the door handle. The comment sucked the air out of me. In front of us, cutting through the rain in the slow lane, a semi-truck contained all of my possessions, all my brother's possessions, and after a yard sale of the junk, all of my parent's stuff. Behind us, living happy lives, my friends: most of the popular girls, many of the jocks, some of the high school band, a few of next years' seniors. I had had some boyfriends. Robert would be a junior, and would probably make all-league as a wide receiver since he started as sophomore on varsity; not that I wanted to get back together.

Behind us I would have probably have made the junior varsity volleyball team even though I wasn't that good. I had a reputation of being "coachable," an annoying yet accurate word, so I usually got decent minutes off the bench. When you move to a new high school no one knows that you are "coachable," now do they? In fact, the coaches probably assume you don't know the new system and you had better have talent to make up for it. Great...

Honestly, I probably wouldn't have tried out for the tennis squad, despite my parents' constant pressure to tryout. I suppose they thought our family matches counted as Wimbledon caliber training. Something about the coordination needed to track and hit a small ball just didn't click with my body.

My hand still gripped the handle a minute later. I had looked forward to going to high school for years, perhaps my whole life, and my father, with no discussion, moved Jimmy, my mother and I. I never said anything to my father about it; he rarely upset me. In fact, he usually doesn't do anything to affect me. I got a taste, one measly year of friendships and memories to last a lifetime and now I had to "start completely anew" and "reinvent."

"What do," surprisingly my voice came out angry, I toned it down, "what do you mean 'reinvent myself?'" My mother slowly adjusted her entire body, her clothes squeaked in her leather seat. She finished turning around and glared at me from the front seat. Her expression more surprised than anything else, "Eleanor. Do not talk to your father that way."

I got my voice under control, "I'm sorry, I am curious. What do you mean?"

His comment showed signs of the infection; surely the moving day was too early for my family to be infected. The pollution is hidden. The tainted objects are not easily noticeable.

From the back seat, I glanced at his eyes in the rearview mirror. My father kept focused like an alcoholic private detective, sleepy eyes deadlocked straight-ahead. I knew he cared about me though.

For as long as I can remember whenever my father got home from work, which could be late, he would come to me and wait until I turned to face him. He'd look at my face as though he was searching for the bunny silhouette crater on a full moon—his eyes first adjusted to the brightness, then the craters became visible, and lastingly he focused on the sincere silhouettes of emotion on my face. He'd ask how I felt and with such patience he could always tell if I was troubled, despite any fudged response. Not that we talked too much if something bothered me; in fact we rarely talked at all, he would simply offer a few positive comments.

I don't blame him for what happened.

During the trip I am sure we passed signs of the horror. Maybe I unconsciously sensed them. Their beginning goes back much further than my experiences.

When we arrived at our new home a second truck was already unloading the heavy furniture. The cold autumn rain fell in heavy drops, almost irritably. My parents asked Jimmy and me to stay out of the way. Since Jimmy already had his bed and some toys he went into his room to play. I went to my new barren room. I stood in the doorway for what must have been twenty minutes.

Moving is a hideous experience. The hardest part of moving was losing friends, one of the most important parts of my life. It's devastating, as if they had died and I was denied the closure of a funeral. What might be worse, or at least more stressful, was the uncertainty of building new friendships. And what for? Our new house felt similar to the last. The suburb and even the city might as well be the same. A city with distinction and character would have been nice: Los Angeles, Chicago, New York or even London. Instead we moved from one listless suburb to another. It's almost like we didn't move at all, just my friends and neighbors have been replaced by strangers. Thankfully I don't have an accent here, but my old friends are a full day's drive away. And I don't have a car. Oh, and I couldn't drive yet.

Eventually, I called Ariel. She answered with an unusually high pitched tone, a sure sign of excitement. Surely, she hadn't been infected yet, excitement is an excellent indicator, depending on the stimulus. She expressed curiosity about the trip and the new house.

"Grass in the front and back, some young trees in the corner, bushes near the house, what you'd expect, it's just like our old place. My room is a little bigger."

"Oh that's nice."

"Honestly, the only highlight is the sliding, like, door-mirror for the closet."

In her somewhat artificial perkiness, she tried to cheer me up, "cool."

"You know, I haven't genuinely looked at myself in a full size mirror."

"I guess I haven't done that too much either."

The new vast distance I traveled lingered in my body. "Ariel, what do you think about the phrase, 'beauty is in the eye of the beholder?'" While she paused to reflect, I sized up my basics in the mirror, here are the measurements: average, average, average, and maybe a little, no maybe too much, no, no that's average too…

Ariel could speak so fast on occasion, "well, I suppose it's like a percentage game in reality. Say forty percent of boys find me somewhat attractive, twenty percent definitely attractive, ten percent incredibly attractive, and five percent just like a total babe," she let out her patented giggle and continued, "while the rest find me dull."

Staring into the mirror the words fell from my mouth, "well my percentages would probably be lower."

"Oh come on Eleanor." Ariel's too sweet to acknowledge her superior looks.

My body gave a slight tremble, "what terrifies you the most Ariel?"

After a brief silence Ariel admitted, "that's a rather dark question."

"I'll tell you what terrifies me."

"What's that?" Ariel's voice embraced the new space between us.

"Nothing is disproportional, nothing is over or underdeveloped on my body, nothing is distinguishing. I have boring hair, dull eyes, like, an average nose, a regular smile with like normal teeth."

"Eleanor, well at least…"

I cut her off, "yeah but, I don't have any freckles, dimples, luscious lips or slim and sexy lips. No long eyelashes or strong jaw or high cheek bones or anything else that would stand out."

"Well isn't that like a good thing, I mean do you want to be like Jeanie Gladwell?" She could have meant two things: Jeanie hit puberty in 5th grade, even the girls made fun of the 'extra arms' coming out of her chest; and nowadays in high school, if she got her weight down a bit, she'd have to shock the boys off her with a Taser.

"Yeah, my body appears to be right on track. It's just that, the end result seems to be more of nothing exciting. My mother's breasts are average, same with grandmas', although it's hard to tell from pictures and like the fact that Mom and Grandma are rather old. At least they're somewhat skinny, for their age I guess."

"So what is it then? You want a distinguishing trait?"

"Exactly."

"Oh yeah, so what about Kelly Talbert?"

"Kelly is such a sweet-heart," I might have been a little upset.

"I was just saying for, like, an example." Kelly has a dark-haired moustache. Big or long nose ok, weird cheeks that's fine, but dark-bushy upper lip… Ariel frequently made me feel better. My body occupied my thoughts a lot and rarely in a positive way.

My mom burst into my room and asked me to get off the phone; the moving men wanted to unload my bed, desk, drawers, and bookshelf. "Mom, come on, it's easy, like my old room." My mom relayed the message to moving men waiting in the hallway behind her.

"Sorry about that." The moving men clambered inside the room with my bed frame and mattress.

"No worries. You reminded me of how much we missed you today in class."

"Oh come on Ariel, I just left," yet I hadn't hung out with Ariel for a week because she had a gymnastics competition (she took second place on the balance beam.) In fact, most of my friends had been gone for at least a few days immediately before my departure. So I never had a going away party with everyone, only afternoons with a few select friends, too-many-days in advance of the actual move for us to admit this was the last time we would see each other.

"At some point today someone gossiped about Darcy and like a ghost I heard what you would have said." Darcy Mainer had always been a mystery to me; or rather her brother. Ariel continued, "you're always so positive about everything; you never speak poorly about other people. That's why everyone loved you."

"Oh come on that's not true."

The moving men noisily entered with another load of my furniture. "Everybody at school truly misses you." A sweet complement, I should have thanked Ariel for giving it, yet a picture of Darcy's brother, Malcolm lingered in my mind. Older, in a not too brotherly way, he's maybe the age of a junior in college, tall but not gangling, broad shoulders yet skinny, piercing blue eyes, big nose, big ears, and big straight white teeth. He still looked attractive in a very masculine way, in my humble opinion. His parents had sent him to a mental institution for a week about a year ago. The details are vague. Apparently he'd become frantic or emotively distressed over sealed plastic bottles. It was all rather sad. Darcy confided to me about feeling a "stigma" for having a mental illness in her family.

After the pause I asked, "my grandparents and parents are skinny, so I should be too, right?"

"Why not?"

"Well Jimmy is a little chubby."

"Yeah, he's like seven."

The moving men came back again with boxes full of my stuff, clothes, and books. On their way out, my mom came in and gave me a dirty look. I gestured for her to calm down, "hey Ariel I need to go, I got my stuff to unpack."

"Oh… Ok, keep in touch, love you."

Once my mom left my room I added, "I think I will give Jamie a call too."

"Oh you haven't spoken with her yet, that's a good idea." Jamie makes up the last third of our trio.

"Love you bye."

"Love you too."

Unpacking all my stuff all at once, I should have been astounded. At the time, I felt hassled, moving my banal and benign stuff. I unpacked toxic substances, materials that could poison so imperceptibly slow that I wouldn't become fully conscious of it. It's funny; people believe it's merely lip-gloss, hair clips, gum, sunglasses, jeans, etc… Although calling those objects by those names is inaccurate, they meant so much more. Putting on a pair of sunglasses is so much more than only wearing sunglasses.

Same with my favorite jeans, it is putting on a personality, an expression of me.

I put in my ear piece and called Jamie while I unpacked. Her speech came through the earpiece level, straight, no high pitched "hel-lo's," no noises or grunts to convey meaning, only a simple typical-Jamie, "hi."

"Hey Jamie."

"How was your trip?"

"Boring." My mom yelled from the hall that pizza would be arriving any minute.

"Where're you getting pizza from?"

"The usual."

"Everyone missed you today at school Eleanor." I organized my clothes in the drawers as they were before.

"Huh, yeah, Ariel told me."

"Suzy might have cried a bit."

"Oh come on."

"I forgot to ask you about your dad's new job." Packing my desk drawers, I had dumped all the stuff into separate plastic grocery bags. Now even the clutter resided in the same spot.

"He's a manager at a bank, Jamie."

"Is that so, Elly," my childhood's name, "L – e" and Jamie knew it, "I mean: what exactly was his promotion?"

"Oh, I am not sure, something with finance."

In a flat tone, "oh really, and he works for a bank?" A little laugh escaped me. Her dry humor worked the same over the phone.

She continued, "well, your father is well-rounded with experience, I'd imagine he could get any kind of promotion." I love it when little Jamie gets so professional.

Smiling, I silently put away some toiletries in the new bathroom. Their specialty is substances that can be applied then absorbed into the body. How much of it had they attempted to infect? Applying hydrochloric acid to my face would have been better. I suppose it's how a person uses the products. Use it correctly and your face won't melt into a deformity you never feel familiar with, no matter how long you stare in the mirror. A deformity not too hideous, just a defect that could be covered up, or compensated for by drawing attention to other aspects of the face, all with a little spell of time and creativity of course.

Jamie gave no indication of annoyance at my inattentiveness. She continued to carry our conversation. "What about your mom?"

"Oh, she recently transferred, but she won't start until next week when we start school."

"So you're not starting school right away?"

"Um, my mom said during the drive that this week we'd stop at some of the stores we passed."

"That's cool."

"They're all the same stores we have back home and we're only getting some missing things around the house."

The pizza had arrived so we said our goodbyes. My parents, Jimmy and I, silently ate native-American-style on the kitchen floor. I remember imagining we were all like Native Americans, except we didn't have a campfire. Returning to my new room was strange; everything lay in the same place as my old home. The door, drawers, bookshelf and bed all rested in the same relations to each other. The difference was the spaces between them, and the huge mirror which doubled the size of the room.

I flicked the lights on and the darkness outside reflected my image in the window. The slightly larger window was similarly placed, although it could have been facing a different direction than before, I never faithfully learned the star constellations. I hadn't a clue which direction Jamie and Ariel slept and I wish I did. I wanted to feel their presence, that sensation of knowing someone is sleeping near you, breathing the same air, experiencing the same temperatures and sounds in their sleep. And if I knew what direction my friends were, despite the distance, I might have experienced that sense of togetherness.

That night I had difficulty falling asleep. When I was

younger I frequently had nightmares; sudden monsters, hairy beasts, shape-shifting murders, mile-long snakes, and of course, all-too-familiar witches. Only the witches would send me to my parents' room for refuge. The witches lingered in my mind after I woke up, waiting to snatch me once I drifted to sleep again. My parents told me the usual "relax, it's only a dream," but of course that doesn't work for small children. I remember my father instructed me to do math because it would wake me up. Addition, subtraction, maybe some multiplication, I must have been Jimmy's age.

My parents failed to understand. I had no problem waking up. What kept me awake was the fact that the witches *knew* where I was and they patiently waited and prepared for my return. I suppose my father tired of me waking him up. So he told me to confront my nightmares so that they would never come back. Any demon or beast, I was to fight, not run away. The problem, of course, is how do you know if you're in a dream? I found out how, and it did work—fighting in dreams at least.

CHAPTER THREE

If I painted a series of paintings of my father, one would be of him drinking coffee, holding a printed newspaper close to his face and a half-eaten piece of toast on a plate in front of him. I never understood that painting of a businessman with a pale green Granny Smith apple in front of his face. If he or the painting supposed to represent an anonymous, straight-and-narrow, probably boring man, or lifestyle, then how come the painting is so abstract? The apple is so conceptual; a newspaper with incomprehensible articles would be so much more accurate of businessmen. Then again, the fact that an abstract object, a giant hovering apple, conveys plenty of meaning, mostly dull facts about the person behind it, says a lot I suppose.

In a painting of my father, a Granny Smith apple would be inappropriate in front of his face. Taste doesn't matter to him, a sour apple, a Honey Crisp, a Macintosh, it doesn't matter. Perhaps a Rome Red would at least elicit a response that it would be better eaten in a pie as opposed to raw. But everyone appreciates that, it's nothing slightly unusual, like enjoying sour apples. And no other object, besides an old fashion printed newspaper, represents my father's anonymity more.

I often asked my father why he insistently reads the newspaper. Most often he replied that he wanted to or it's important to understand what's going on in the world. As I got older I once asked him why it's important because he can't change any of it. Invariably he would ask if I was worried about some specific crisis; the chemical spill, the children in the burnt factory, the hostilities between two minor nations. I would remind him that I don't follow the news, and then he would go ahead and tell me not to be worried. To finish our conversation, my father would comment about how reading the news is also important to be able to intelligently converse with co-workers and clients. The conversations needed to be apolitical, especially with clients. Nevertheless people like to chat and hear other's ideas and feelings about certain problems and, occasionally, their possible solutions. Then, without a cruel smirk, or a pause for thought, he would go back to hiding behind the morning paper.

What about people expressing ideas or feelings that have nothing to do with anything in newspapers? I failed to ask, his reply too foreseeable: that would be unprofessional. He might ask if I felt alright and give me his searching look, but setting down the paper even then would be doubtful.

Every day he has the identical posture while reading the papers; I could paint the finishing touches on his hands any morning of the year. Speaking through the paper does nothing to mask his deep voice, "hey Eleanor, would you like to make some money tomorrow night?" Without waiting for a response he continued "they're having a focus group for eleventh and twelfth graders from the area, fifty dollars for two hours."

"I guess."

"Come on, you could meet kids from the area."

"But Dad, I'm only a sophomore."

"Yes, well, I doubt it matters that much, I'll give them a call."

The next day, during the middle of the week, my father and I drove to the business district of the suburb. Mom wasn't working, yet Father came home early. I wasn't sure what to expect, I hadn't started school yet. Would people be any different here, would the styles be the same…? My father told me not to worry; they only pay me for my opinions.

The building, outside and in, gave the impression of an underpaid and uninspired architect. We stopped on the fourth floor, walked down a narrow hallway to the last door, and entered a long comfortable room. Lamps hung on the brick walls projecting white lights onto the ceiling, not too bright, not too harsh. A mirror ran the length of one wall. At the far end of the room some ten teenagers lounged on several couches.

A lady greeted us. Normal height, shoulder-length light brown hair and hazel eyes, her name is Macy. She appeared gently attractive in her high heels, black slacks, and a soft maroon blouse. She asked me to fill out a short form. When I gave it back she clacked her lips and frowned as she read it over. "You're not in our age group tonight."

"No." My father had told me not to lie or otherwise

worry about the age requirement.

"My family and I have recently moved here from… and I thought this would be an excellent opportunity for Elly to meet some new friends." The group of high-schoolers sat so far down the hallway-of-a-room that a normal speaking tone would have been hard to hear. Unfortunately, my father's deep voice carries.

"Yes, but we want a specific age group."

Booming, "Elly is very articulate and opinionated…"

Long gazes started coming from the couches so I waited for an opportunity to give my father's clothes a quick yank. Suddenly, Michelle appeared from a hidden room along the mirrored wall. Wearing some orange flats, Michelle is also average height. She has long, layered, dark brown hair, a strategic brilliant smile and contemplative brown eyes. With her tight blue jeans and a stylish red blouse, many men must find her attractive, although she is rather average, if it's at all possible to get past her amazing smile. Everything had an ordinary appearance, even her lips were naturally moist, no lipstick. She approached us eyes down, found my shoes, looked up at me, then to Macy and finally to my father, giving him a quick flash of her white teeth which faded to a simple yet pleasant smile.

Macy handed her the card I filled out. Michelle articulated my name slowly and sweetly with a touch of dignity, but no snobbishness, "Eleanor," an intonation my mom probably had in mind when she named me. "What do you like to go by?"

"Eleanor, please," true, although if it wasn't, her pronunciation would have changed my mind.

"Do you have a cell phone Eleanor? Tonight we will be discussing a few electronics."

I would like to have shown her my cell phone, but it's a bit bulky and old.

"Yes."

"May I see it?"

"Sure," I took it out of my light jacket. Trying not to sound too apologetic I added, "I usually use my headset. My hair covers it up so I hold my cell like this," I moved to a pose, "so people can see that I'm on a cell phone." The pose also minimizes the bulkiness.

Michelle gave me a closed-lipped smile and continued, "did you pick this out?"

"Of course." Looking her in the eyes and speeding up my speech, "over a year ago, but Dad is getting me a new one for my birthday next summer," I finished with a big smile at Dad. If Michelle realized she asked a dumb question, she hid it.

With a relaxed elegance, she smiled and shook hands with my father, then me, "my name is Michelle Meyer." What a smooth introduction, no hesitation or foolish attempt at some perceived youthful handshake. Her soft hand gave off a slight aroma of a melon lotion.

"Where did you move from again?"

My father said the suburb followed by the city. Michelle excused herself and Macy to go into the hidden backroom. I could barely perceive parts of their conversation over my dad's comments.

"She is wearing—"

Happily, my father started in, "I told you hon…"

"—age-compression—"

My dad continued, "…your age wasn't an issue…"

"—from sector—" my dad went rambling on, but I could still hear fragments, "—she's a setter!" or did

Michelle say, "spreader"?

My father droned on with his booming voice and I inched forward to the room. I couldn't hear anything for a while and then Macy came out, shocked at my closeness. I managed to take a few steps back before Michelle walked out of the room.

"We do have a spot available if you would like to join us."

"Yes."

"Mr. Callan, if you…"

"Please, just Roger."

"Roger, please return at eight-thirty, we should be finished by then."

My father left and Macy and I walked to the over-stuffed couches. About ten of us sat on four couches arranged into more of a circle than square. Half the participants were guys. Macy and Michelle sat on a love seat blocking our exit. Note pads rested in their laps. In-between the window and a couch, they set a table with some snacks, a vegetable dip plate and bottled water.

Macy started, "hello, my name is Macy and this is Michelle. We work for a marketing and research agency called *Incantando* and we asked you to join us tonight to give us your opinions. Please feel free to say what is on your mind—we are not your parents—we only ask that you be respectful of the other participants. Feel free to get up at any time and help yourself to a snack or a drink."

The other participants appeared attentive although clueless. All of us were naïve. Nobody had a firm idea of the crime we would commit. About half the participants joined their ranks that night, drinking the sealed water bottles.

Macy continued, "let's go around and introduce ourselves. Please say what vegetable you would be if you had to be one and why."

Some of the participants smiled at each other, some gazed at the ceiling, and one or two stared out the window. I thought it a bit stupid too. Michelle took some notes. Macy answered her own question, perhaps a little too excited, "I'd be a Brussels sprout because that way nobody would want to eat me."

"That's an interesting ice breaker Macy." Michelle's smile quickly faded, "hmm, wheat because it's a staple, yet can be made into, like, an amazing variety of foods." I ended up choosing a carrot because it helps people with vision. After the entire group contributed to the geeky salad ice breaker, the bizarre questions continued.

"This is open to anyone, please say what you think as it comes to mind. If Coke were a person, who would it be?" Nobody moved. Finally a guy with an awkward posture guessed, a country singer starlet.

I thought I could do better than that, "well, right now, Coke would be…" and I named a leading male film actor.

Michelle chimed in "what about a few years ago?"

"Perhaps," I suggested a leading female model/film actress and added, "but that is only my opinion."

Michelle had a few follow up questions to support my opinions. As I answered, she and Macy scribbled more notes. Macy then asked about drinking soda. What brands did people like? When did we drink it, time of day, events, certain meals, with friends? After a while Macy handed out pins and papers with various logos on it; however, none of the logos represented soda. "Please circle the cool brands."

After finishing that task, Macy gave us some full-page

ads torn out from magazines, except the pages were without any tears and single sided. Again the ads contained no soda nor any of the logos from the last task. One advertised a cell phone though.

"Please circle the parts of the ads that are not *authentic.*"

I believe the first marketed shoes. After a minute we discussed what we had circled in the ad. They took notes. How these activities had anything to do with the coming infection, I had not a clue.

The highlight of the night had to do with music. Macy asked where and how we enjoyed listening to music. I said it depended on my mood, location, and what genre of music I wanted to listen to. Michelle then asked me what five groups I listened to the most at the moment. I listed one mainstream band and the rest were underground or simply lesser known. Everyone was freely giving their opinions and the group erupted in comments and conversation. Some talked about one of the bands; others asked me about the group from New York or Chicago. At that moment, I saw how wide Michelle's smile could get. She calmed the group and asked some more questions. She only asked me about musical taste.

The focus group ended with a very specific instance. My father came into the room and Michelle told Macy to "please take care of him." Because of the angle of the couch I saw my father and Macy talking, although I could only hear my father of course. Why couldn't he wait on the first floor lobby like everyone else's parents, instead of embarrassing me further? But now I only wish he wasn't infected.

"Oh, I'm sorry. I'll go back down." My father took a step backward, but Macy asked him another question.

"Sure, I'd love a coffee."

Macy went into the backroom behind the mirror and came out with a cup. She quickly opened and poured all of a creamer into his coffee. My father didn't notice anything odd. His face was hidden when he took a sip because Macy and he walked to the backroom. About five minutes later we finished and my father threw his coffee away before we left. He has not been the same since.

CHAPTER FOUR

Infection, spells, Agency, "they," et cetera... are concepts which evolved for me from vague organisms floating in a primordial soup to blubbering dinosaurs and eventually into large-brained creatures with opposable thumbs who are, hopefully, not the end of evolution. Like so many ideas or events, the history, development, and evolution are important and even instrumental for understanding. And one has to know one's enemy before they can ever defeat them. My experience is all I am sure of, "they" were certainly here before me. Admittedly, I am not even entirely sure of my own experiences. When I started school in my new city I still floated in the soup, yet thanks to my father's "reinvent" comment, I began to become more complex, a multi-celled organism if you will.

His prediction about the focus group came true too; I did make friends. Two of the girls approached me after everything was over; I wonder if they entered my number wrong though because I never heard from them, and I foolishly forgot to ask for their numbers. I don't think they went to the same high school as me. The next day I would have another chance though. I started school. With only a few weeks left in the first semester, making friends during my second semester before summer and my junior year wouldn't be easy.

My mom dropped me off as the first bell rang and hurriedly pointed out the sign for the office. Mom's only advice, utterly predictable having heard it infinite times before, "be positive." Anticipating my arrival, an office assistant speedily escorted me to my first classroom: history, a perfect subject for such a grey hour. Instead of fluttering butterflies, my stomach ached with a sickening feeling of pending food poisoning.

While the tardy bell blared, we entered the classroom. The office assistant and teacher had a moment of confusion. Everyone already seated, they fixed their eyes on me, a spectacle arriving late. Rather than telling me the location of my seat, the teacher first told the office assistant my seat location and then she told me my seat—awkward.

I noticed a human phenomenon standing awkwardly before the class that morning. This phenomenon of human nature, if humans even have a nature, is to judge with a short deliberation. Looking out at the class, dozens of pairs of inquisitive eyes stared at me, starting at my head, then various features of my face, and quickly scanning my whole person and clothes, even my shoes, rendering a judgment with a smile, frown, eye-roll or scoff in about thirty seconds or less. At my old high school, I had known most of my peers for many years, back to elementary school, so this phenomenon never occurred. I suppose it happens to everyone, if not a new school, then a new job. For me this was my first inspection, or so I thought.

The tall teacher, Mr. Swords, wore his dark wavy hair stiff and his shorts way-too-short, both for the weather and his hairy legs. True to fashion, he was extremely loud, testosterone saturated, and active. Some of the black hairs on his legs had to be over an inch long. He taught US history with a genuine zeal, striding erratically around the classroom. I found out later that he also taught a PE class, and all kinds of rumors swirled as to why he only had one PE class now.

In a deep bass voice even louder than my father's, he announced "we have a new student with us today." I grew tense sensing an expectation from me. Why couldn't he simply announce a new student in a more casual manner?

"Eleanor Callan, all of us offer you a warm welcome. Please stand up and tell us a little bit about yourself." I gave him a puzzled expression trying to question his seriousness—what is the point of standing and saying, "I like long walks on the beach..."

Oblivious to my expression, he continued, speaking directly to me as if I was a deaf-mute, "where you are coming from, what interests do you have, what do you like to *do*?" The last part almost sounded like an accusation.

Heat rushed to my face; no doubt I blushed bright red. Standing up took a while as I peeled myself from my seat, "hello, I'm happy to meet all of you." I tried to focus on few faces, like they tell you when you publicly speak, pick out four faces in different areas of the room. That didn't work when the entire class remained one big blur of bored and judgmental eyes.

"Um, I like what most girls like I guess. I enjoy playing

tennis, um, I like movies, shopping, hanging out with friends…" I flopped down. Looking back at the experience, I am glad when I flopped down I actually landed in my seat. However, at the time, I felt embarrassed and thought—how unnatural?

"Thank you Eleanor. Do you play doubles?"

I simply smiled, unsure he was asking a question. After a pause he finally moved on with roll call. Only then did I realize I failed to mention volleyball. In a way I felt I ruined the last of what little chance I had of making the team. The rest of class was a haze with an exception of Mr. Swords' livid outburst. During the middle of class, standing in front of the chalk board, Mr. Swords became irritated, "you should be taking notes people! When I write on the board it *means* something: it's important information you should learn and contemplate." I had teachers like him before. The teachers who believe in the power of the pen, or, rather, the chalk. What is written is important! In fact, I had classmates like this before too, except now I had no idea who any of them were.

Some girls approached me in-between classes. "Mr. Swords is such a geek, I like can't believe he had you do that."

"He totally put you on the spot."

"Did he tell you what he planned to do?"

"No, not at all."

"He is so weird. Do you like his hairy legs?"

The girls all giggled and I did too.

"He used to only teach PE but some people say he was too gay…"

"…or too much of an exhibitionist."

Everyone let out a laugh at my comment. They

introduced themselves; I couldn't remember all their names at first. After the next class we had a break and I discovered the locations of my next classes. Once I found the last one, I had no idea what to do.

I found myself sitting alone, a rather unnatural situation. Earlier, a young man had floated a question of what I thought of the school, only to answer it himself by saying the design came from a prison. I had thought he was just another odd angst-ridden teenager, another word I don't much care for "angst," although it accurately captures the first impression of this peer. He could have been correct. The school is square and the second story forms a solid square. The four entrances are located at the sides of the square at ground level. The main entrance has a gate, but it wouldn't be hard to install three more gates to enclose the central yard. The windows are too large for a prison, but then again installing bars would be easy. And the windows only open from the top anyway. The administration building, placed a little off center in the yard, wouldn't make much sense in a prison; they would be surrounded by a sea of convicts in the yard. The comment sounded too typical since all the young adults are stuck here. Of course, after eighteen years of age, that magical age, students can get kicked out of high school and also have the option of quitting.

Jamie's dad once explained to us, "the purpose of high school isn't to learn anything, that's college in this nation; high school is for discipline. If you fail to graduate you're out of luck, you can't even become a dishwasher. A third-world foreigner who sneaks into the country to escape enslavement to the local mafia could be a dishwasher here. If you're born here and fail high school, well, sorry this business has rules too and it's obvious you can't follow them. Or you lack the minimum determination and discipline required to wipe scraps from porcelain. Maybe try your luck at ditch digging…but I still think you need a high school diploma to do that if you're born here."

I wondered how happy those eighteenth birthdays are once the person has a "quit-or-get-kicked-out" conversation with the principal.

"Hey Thug Toni!" the principal's smile immediately throws Toni off-guard. He's never seen the principal smile. And even more surprising, is his, are they, yes, his teeth are crooked in the identical way as his own! Those teeth had started many fights for Toni, and he had sized the principal up before, he seemed big, but no scars on his fist, unlike his own. "So here's the deal Toni, I'm going to make you an offer you cannot refuse."

I giggled and abruptly checked myself: giggling by myself on bench in the middle of the courtyard… For the second occasion that day I could feel my cheeks blushing, nobody knew my personality yet. Luckily the bell rang and I could hurry to class.

Happily, I had a group of girls to sit with during lunch. They fired a few questions at me, everyone would listen and then, much to my relief, the conversation veered to more familiar topics. Everyone seemed exceedingly nice. I couldn't join in the conversations too much. A great deal of the talk centered on what people had said or done.

By the end of the day I had made the acquaintances of a lot of girls and a few boys. Some of them were incredibly cute, but I wanted to focus on friends and school first. One stood out among the rest.

Mark and I didn't meet on my first day, but I found out

his name. The most distinct aspect about Mark, although it's only a trait to notice if he isn't looking, are his muscular forearms and nice veins. I certainly wouldn't compliment him, "hey you," give head nod, "nice veins," but it's true. At first glance, anyone would notice Mark's steely, cobalt blue eyes and dark chocolate hair. He wears his hair slightly messy, a way a person who is creative, quiet, and attractive-but-still-sensitive would. He also has a faintly visible vein running up the middle of his bicep and appears to be rather capable.

When Mark and I saw each other, we comfortably kept eye-contact and smiled in chorus. I had an inexpressible moment; the draw of the tide to the moon, the singular sound of a nervous and excited heart, the complete absences of other people around, love at first sight!? But it never is—they open their mouths and everything tumbles downhill so quick you even forget the sensation when you first saw them. So I did the smartest thing I could after Mark and I made eye-contact, I walked away and didn't talk to him. At least this way I could prolong the feeling a bit longer and let my imagination run.

My mom picked me up from school. I told her the positive highlights of the day; she seemed pleased, "see, you just have to be positive. People are attracted to that." When we got home my mom made me a snack and we walked to Jimmy's school and back. From then on, I would walk alone to Jimmy's elementary school daycare and we would go home together.

Mother made me spend time with Jimmy since he had no friends in our new town. Well, neither did I. My little kid brother, what can I say. Jimmy's schedule rotates around eating, sleeping and the computer. He's a little chubby around the belly and the cheeks, yet the resemblance is undeniable, despite my constant recollections about the adoption agency.

"Oh boy, I still remember how Mom looked at you. You completely covered in your own drool. She thought you were so cute she couldn't resist rescuing you from the orphanage." I think I had him convinced for a few months when he was five. His belief got so intense, I almost felt bad about it. Hours after I had teased him and after he had brushed his teeth, about the point all I thought about was my elephant, he had approached our father. "Dad, you are my daddy, right?" Poor little Jimmy probably thought I was out of earshot too.

Jamie gave me an elephant figurine in elementary school. Her father sort of had his own little custom which he passed to Jamie, and Jamie to me. I keep the elephant figurine on my bedroom windowsill. The elephant is made of some hardwood, painted black with some white for the tusk, eyes, and nails. Every night immediately before I start getting ready for bed, so long as I don't need to hurry, I sit and contemplate the day. Elephants have excellent memories. I determine if any part of my day did not go the way I wanted. Then I determine if the event was within or outside of my control. If an experience went poorly and I could have changed it by my attitude or actions, I face the elephant inward until I figure out how or what I should change to improve my situation. According to Jamie, if I am happy with my day or the undesirable aspects of the day are beyond my control, I face the elephant to the window to dream. I also imagine the elephant gazes at the stars to determine the true extent of control over the undesirable. Jamie sometimes keeps her elephant behind a picture frame for privacy from her parents. I left mine in the open, nobody at my house knows what it means besides me.

After Jimmy questioned my parents enough about the adoption, both of them talked to me. I had to tell Jimmy the truth. So I pulled Jimmy aside after dinner the next day and he wouldn't believe me! He knew our parents made me say that I had lied earlier. I took him to the bathroom mirror and we stared at ourselves. I pointed out our similar features; we have the same tone and thickness of brown hair, our eyes are identical in shape and shade of brown. Jimmy's answer: Mom and Dad searched for a kid who matched them and me.

So I had to take a step back. "How come you think that I said you're adopted?"

"Because you don't like me and want me to feel bad."

I turn to face him directly, "James, I like you, you're my brother, and I was only teasing you because it's funny."

James kept looking at me through the mirror, "yeah, real funny…"

"Well, so what if you're an orphan? That liberates you."

James had no response. I didn't even grasp what I was suggesting.

"Besides, how come our parents insist that you're their baby?"

"They love me and don't want to hurt me."

"They do love you, so wouldn't they tell you the truth?"

"I guess so."

"Of course they would tell you the truth, that way you can make your own decisions."

I satisfied Jimmy's skepticism. Regrettably, through the

experience I realized how typical I am. And my commonality to the common people penetrates deeper than my outward appearance. I had no distinction at birth or origin either; my brother proved that. I didn't abruptly emerge on earth under extraordinary circumstances. No one mysteriously discovered me wrapped in a blanket in a secluded forest wearing nothing but a locket. I didn't become an orphan through miraculously surviving a major natural disaster. My mother didn't die giving birth to me, thankfully. My common birth is why I fail to believe in destiny. Most of my life I waited for a mysterious uniqueness to be revealed to me so that I could have a destiny, a purpose of solving that mystery. Ordinary has no path, to greatness or despondency.

Perhaps in the future Jimmy would decide to keep his chubbiness. Who cares if it's the wrong kind of distinction? Although, looking around, it seems like the older people get, the more normal a chubby person becomes.

When it comes to temperament, Jimmy and I are not too similar. It's such a horrible thing to admit, but if people were able to willingly join "them," Jimmy would be one of the first in line. He constantly plays computer games and watches TV.

Coming home from the first day at our new schools, I tried to play with him. I knew some of his interests so I asked if he wanted to play wizards.

"No, Mom hasn't bought me the wand yet."

"We'll get sticks from the yard."

Annoyed at my ignorance he spat, "those don't *do anything* Elly," and he continued clicking at the screen.

I mocked him, "well what do the store wands *do*?"

He remained hutched over the computer desk, "I don't know, Mom hasn't bought it yet, I think they like make sounds and stuff."

"Alright, we'll make sounds ourselves, *phew, phew, phew*."

He stared at the screen. No sense of humor. I went back to my room, and before long my mother came by, "Eleanor, what are you doing?"

"Mom he doesn't want to play with me, he's being a little brat on the internet."

She continued my sentence, "...then play with him on the internet."

The fact that the internet is kinda single-player failed to deter my mom. I went back into the living room; it's "open concept," the living space and kitchen are together, no walls separate them. I pulled up a chair next to the computer desk at the far end of the living room. His demeanor slightly changed, Mom must have prepped him for me.

"So what's up James?"

He glanced over at me, "you're lucky I just found out about a new play site."

"Oh yeah,"

"Yeah, Todd told me about it." He was messaging with his friends from our old city. South Park songs played on YouTube, however Jimmy wasn't watching them. Lastly and most actively, he played a cookie racing game on a cookie brand's website. I assumed he turned the sound off for the game. James excelled at computers. In a few more years he would grasp more than me.

He opened the link from Todd, "whoa!"

Some animated pastel nonsense bounced around the screen, "so what's this?"

"It's like a world and you get a person to like move around and stuff."

He signed up and had to answer so many questions I volunteered to type for him. "No, James, that's not right, don't do your birthday like that, let me do it," of course he wouldn't let me. He only wanted to get through it, "whatever," his new favorite word. At least he got the year right. Although Mom's expectation of "playing internet together," was a bit ludicrous, I was grateful for the opportunity to get to know my brother. I could go over his preferences with him.

James favorite color: blue, second choice: green. If he could be an animal he would be a tiger. Why? James skipped the question because the site had no dropdown menu; they expected a user to type the answer. I would find out anyways because he couldn't sign in without completing all the questions. So why tigers? "Cool." The last toy he got: a computer game. Which one: Penguin something. Favorite food: pizza; drink: soda. I can't recall the rest: movies, snack food, sports to watch, sports to play, etc.... Finally he finished, although he played it many other occasions and the website required him to answer more questions to get access to other parts of the game.

"Sweet!" James's avatar was a tiger. He could move around and then talk with other animals, shop for things, and play some silly games. The game was interesting, but not engaging, a little too young for me. After not saying anything to each other for five minutes, I decided I had played enough internet with him. As soon as I got up the phone rang.

My mom announced from the hallway, "here honey, the phone is for you."

"Really?" My friends would call my cell.

"It's a Michelle, from the agency yesterday."

"Alright, I got it in here Mom!"

I connected with a push, "hello?"

"Hello, Eleanor?" Her voice filled the room.

"Yes"

"This is Michelle from *Incantando*, we met two days ago." Was I hearing her in both ears? "I would like to interview you for a potential job. It's like a reporter position."

"Um, Ok."

"I need to interview you for the position to make sure that we are the right fit though, in person."

"Oh, Ok," it sounded like she was in person with me already.

"During our focus groups we meet some cool young people, who understand what is going on. I thought you were articulate, and like, well you seem to be a cool person."

"Um, thanks, I'm flattered, what would you like me to do?"

"Umm, it's like better if we discuss everything in person. I am leaving for New York in like two days and then to LA a few days after that, argh, it's really hectic. Are you available tomorrow evening, say six-thirty?"

"Yes but…"

"Great, do you mind if I talk to your mom about the job and like getting downtown and everything. We would do the interview at our offices," a touch of seriousness hung in her expression, "in the city, not where we met before."

"Sure."

When I handed my mom the phone she reacted normally, despite the intensity and clarity of Michelle's voice. She made a series of "ah-huh's" and "Ok's" and "Sure's." After she beeped the phone off, I regained my composure and gave her my puppy-dog-face, patent pending.

"Well it's part-time. I'm not clear on what you'd be doing, she definitely likes your opinion. So you want to do this?"

"Yes!"

"Well, she said she would be happy to meet you tomorrow."

"Thanks Mom!"

"She'll text me the address and floor number and then I need you to find directions on the internet."

My father's absence at dinner made the new house feel more customary. Right before I went to sleep, he opened the front door. For some reason my father neglected to give me his sincere, patient and intent look while he asked me how I felt. He only said goodnight through the door.

I had difficulty falling asleep even though I lay on my old mattress. The spaces between my furniture, the distance to the walls, the ceiling hanging over my head, all the space tossed and turned me as I tried to fall asleep.

Like the gradual sound of morning traffic, the sound of my parents arguing reached my room. Thankfully the new house muffled their words. Yet an ugly noise of anger, the desperate sound of my upset mother penetrated the walls.

Eventually, I relaxed and once again sleep crept into my body. Unhappily some words made their way to my room, waking me once more. My mom yelled, "you're so inconsiderate to Eleanor and Jimmy! How can you not think about them?!" I couldn't help myself and let out a chuckle: thanks for waking me Mom, how considerate. Although the arguing was not too unusual, my father had changed since he had the creamer from the Agency.

The next day at school blurred by pretty much the same as the first. I started to put faces to names, but I still missed a lot of insider jokes, well, like all of them. The day flew by. To be honest, all I thought about was the interview with Michelle later in the day. What would they have me do? Review ads like we did at the focus group? Modeling? I'm not that attractive, but maybe they judged differently. I'm certainly not ugly. I guess I could be a model if I had the air blowing through my hair and all the makeup, new clothing, lights and everything. Maybe I would create the ad. What would the interview be like?

My mom finally pulled into the driveway at five-thirty, in a few more moments my interview would induct me into the Agency. Only my mom and I would be going, Jimmy stayed at the daycare until we came back. I had no idea I would become a part of the conspiracy. My part eludes me. Are people needed who are not infected under their spell?

CHAPTER FIVE

I wanted a job so much. I would meet people, have something to put on college resumes, and some spending money. My mom took a long time to get ready, and she just got home from work. Waiting in the car, the sun lowered before me; autumn came to an end, and winter's chill blew. Darkness would descend on downtown before our arrival.

We drove in silence, stopping and starting on the suburban streets. Halfway, speeding on the expressway, my mom gave me some last second help and nervousness. "Job interviews have a few questions they always ask. It might help if you start mulling them over."

"Sure."

As we advanced downtown, with the sun setting behind us, the skyscrapers stood against the darkest part of the twilight sky. Journeying to the downtown area of a city is a little intimidating, knowing everything happening, and witnessing the filth of humanity openly displayed. The rancid homeless people in the open, certainly on drugs, forsaken by family and friend, more of them have to be close, coiled up in abandoned buildings, lonely and desperate. And the drugs in general, altering people so they can go to expensive clubs and ignore the vagrants they never assume they will become. The crimes, the prostitution, the violence, it happens in the suburbs too, but without a doubt, at the exact moment we entered the city, they occurred here.

The tall buildings, identical to our old city yet rearranged, reminded me of a time we approached our old city from a different highway, a questioning of being lost oscillating with feelings of familiarity. I wanted to make these buildings recognizable, and when I could, the sense of worry diminished some. Still too far to reflect the cloudless sunset behind us, the grey buildings fought against the landscape they dominated. Somewhere in the city a man plotted murder against a friend who wronged him.

"They will want to hear about your previous jobs and responsibilities so mention the baby sitting you've done. And mention Jimmy, you've been babysitting him for close to two years now."

Normally, I would just nod, but she was driving. "Yeah."

"And they will probably ask you a question like: what are your two best qualities? And when you are finished answering, they will follow up with what are your two worst qualities, or two qualities that you hope to improve upon, or two negative qualities, alright?"

"Ok."

"But you can't just say anything. You need to make those negative attributes positive."

"Um sure… er."

"So, like, I need to have a clean office before I work."

"Alright," why couldn't she change "office" to "room." As lame as it sounded, I realized I would probably use the answer, it was true. The question is rather ridiculous anyways.

"They'll probably ask you why you want the job."

"Ok, but like, I haven't a clue what the job is about."

We drove close enough to the buildings that their height still impressed, although, since nightfall, only artificial lights illuminated the streets with a pale yellow color. "I believe she mentioned a reporter position."

"Oh yeah, that's right. Um, what do you suppose that means?"

"Well… it's a right turn once we're off, right Elly?"

Without referring to the directions in my hand, "yes."

"You'll probably have to do some writing."

The car windows cut the buildings into giant blocks. I couldn't stop searching the scene outside our car, as if I sought a person, or a thing. Would it be so bad to live in the city? So many more possibilities existed.

Eventually, we pulled into a building's underground parking lot. The sound of the engine became so much more apparent. Even the grip of the tires became discernible on the turns. Although it was close to six thirty, we still had to descend to the second level to find parking.

The office buzzed with activity, long past working hours. We entered a comfortable waiting room furnished with azure patterned couches and seats. Two coffee tables laid with colorful glossy magazines anchored the two couches. A small empty receptionist desk did little to block the view of the hall where several men and women silently turned a corner. A little blond haired woman asked us to wait. As noiselessly as she came, she left even less perceptibly.

Neither my mother nor I picked up any magazines. My mother sat up straight, her back inches off the seat. With a sense of urgency, she checked her phone; it hadn't rung. She told me she'd meet me in the office or the car if she wasn't back when I finished. She had to make a call.

I waited about ten minutes and finally decided to find the restroom. Passing the empty receptionist desk, I ventured into the hall. Taking a right was my only choice. I saw the restrooms, but I couldn't help but notice an indigo light escaping under a door at the end of the hall. The hallway turned left after the door. A woman emphasized talking points in a sweet yet slightly slurry voice, "sealed drinks," "carbonated drinks," "soda." Like a speech in a sports movie, I could only hear the peaks of sentences, not the low valleys of the speech. "Diffusion," "epidemic," "this is it folks," the pronouncements flickered in and out of my consciousness.

I inched closer to the glowing room. The indigo light remained constant, and a slight vibration shook me. I started to stretch to peek inside the room when clear and concise words froze me in place.

"We are sending out a virus. We target tweens to teenagers. First we go against this target, only then do we go against others. In order for the virus to be successful, we first require an effective stealth campaign, before anything else."

A flat screen hung on the wall immediately to the right. Instinctively, I glanced to my right down the hallway, and peeking around the corner, not more than ten feet away stood a staring man. As I turned to face him, he slithered around the corner and strode right at me. I shouldered out of the way. He went into the room, and with a swift violent gesture he jerked the door open and then shut, slowing only at the end to not slam it. The door almost noiselessly clicked shut.

My apology still stuck in my throat, I stared at the closed door for a few seconds. The waiting room was my only option and no sooner than I sat down did Macy appear. She wore a grey woman's business suit with a white blouse. With an all-too-normal smile she spoke with a sense of urgency, "hey Eleanor, why-don't-cha come back with me to Michelle's office."

I got up once more. Macy waited for me in the hallway, but once I crossed the threshold she took off with rapid short strides in her skirt. I nearly jogged to catch-up. She hurried me past the conference room and restrooms, rounding the corner without changing her stride.

To my surprise, the hallway extended further and came to a "T" where we took a left. Having gained so much ground sprinting in the hall, Macy waited with her arm extended holding a door open for me.

"Please take a seat. Michelle will be with you shortly."

Immediately before I entered the door, Macy hurried back down the hall leaving the door open. Turning and entering the room, I first noticed my reflection in the window. I took a few steps forward; the inside lights drowned out the stars and blackness outside. No other buildings blocked the view so high. Michelle's large black desk imposed itself on the room. A large flat screen monitor sat in one corner and a picture frame in the other.

Nothing else was on the desk, not even a keyboard. Through the reflection in the window I noticed the picture frame was absolutely blank.

I took a seat in one of the two black leather seats. On the wall hung a large black and white photograph, a skinny naked young woman standing and covering herself up with her arms and hands. Her feet pointed inward, she barely bent over to cover herself up. Wind blew her hair high up above her head. I couldn't stop staring at her unabashed expression. She was screaming, flashing her white teeth, yet her lips and high-bony cheeks smiled, her eyes fixed on me.

Michelle quickly walked in and broke the staring contest, "oh-my-gosh, Eleanor how are you?"

"Uh, good."

She quickly sat down in her black leather chair and swiveled to face me. "Would you like anything to drink?" The back of her seat came up to the same height as her head. She got up and removed her suit jacket.

"No thanks."

A keyboard slid out from under the desk and the screen awoke from hibernation. "It's like such a drawback to this business; you have to make your clients happy." She finished hanging up her suit jacket in a corner. "This guy today, he goes, 'could we move back the meeting another—'," she cut herself off, sat down again and leaned forward. Changing her tempo, she said, "you seem nervous. Or are you pissed off?"

I mumbled a no.

"I don't blame you. Here I am making excuses for being late, bad form on my part. I'm sorry."

"Oh, it's…" I made a face indicating, "it's no big deal."

Michelle gave me a soft smile back, "hey, I downloaded some *Charlotte Gainsbourg* you mentioned at the focus group." She gazed into her screen and clicked the mouse. From speakers in the top corners of the office came the rising sounds of guitars.

"I just started listening to her, so far it's amazing."

I glanced at the speaker in front of me to the top left of Michelle's head. When my eyes came back to Michelle she was smiling at me. I finally leaned back in my seat.

"I would say that we should get started, but in truth we've been sort of interviewing since I first met you. I would like to have a normal conversation with you, like two people meeting, except that you'll probably talk a lot more than you normally would when meeting a new adult," her eyes widened and she smirked, "who'd bore you talking about themselves." Looking behind Michelle at the reflection of her in the window, her picture frame illuminated with a portrait of several smiling women. My muscles relaxed, the chair started to mold to my body.

Michelle let the music continue to play. She asked about my favorite movie and then told me hers. She asked me about my favorite scene and why I enjoyed it so much. All the while the colors of pictures illuminated the window: beach vacation, girl's night out, bridesmaid with friends (her fingers were bare), sidewalk with a dog, etc…

"What's the way to achieve happiness?"

"Well, um…"

"Don't worry; I'm not expecting you to solve the world's problems. What's your initial reaction?"

"Well I guess it depends on the person."

"Ok, what about you?"

"Well, friends, having new experiences."

"What kind of experiences?"

"Um, positive ones."

"Give me a few examples."

I checked her electronic photo frame again and Michelle realized it. "Ah, fun experiences, like parties, having adventures, weddings, falling in love."

"Next question: what do you sense binds all people together?"

The expression on my face made her rephrase.

"So like what brings people together?"

Again I could only make a filler response while I thought about it. Michelle smiled and went back to staring at her computer screen.

"I'm not too sure, I mean, everyone's an individual. Well my friends and I have similar interests, we like the same shows, playing tennis, music and stuff like that."

"Which one of those activities binds you together the most?"

I contemplated for some time. "Well I guess, I met my girlfriends at school, so, like everything to do with school binds us together."

"Can you recall a situation where you investigated something, anything at all, like where someone got an idea from or who first started a trend?"

My muscles tighten again for a moment. I peeked again at the reflection of her electronic picture frame. "Research, that wasn't for school or anything, it's ok if you can't remember anything now."

A new picture flashed behind Michelle of a snowy mountain landscape with her and a friend in the center. "Oh, last fall I did some searching on the internet for scarves, not for shopping, how to wear them."

"Please tell me more."

"My friends and I would bundle our hair up in scarves in the late fall or sometimes in winter when it's the right temperature. My Indian friend wouldn't ever do it though, she said it's too old school, a way her mom would wear it. Her parents are from India, but she's American."

"So you found pictures of people from India wearing scarves?"

"The Middle East, Iran I believe. The women are so beautiful and the variety of colors and styles is amazing. I ended up getting a silk scarf. It's best to wear with thick black framed glasses."

Michelle typed for a moment. "As far as appearances go, Ok, so just like," she gestured from her face to her body, "what the world sees—what are the top three things that you want to make sure look good?" Michelle had on a white sleeveless blouse. She wore her hair down. It brushed her shoulders and rested behind her back.

"Well, I suppose my hair is the most important." She had been asking why to every question so I kept going, "people almost always notice it."

"And second?"

"Hmm, I would say clothing cause, because again, people almost always see it, and clothing gives a sense of presentation. Lastly would be like, a personal fashion sense. So not only nice clothing but a sense of theme, season, showing who you are, that sort of thing."

"Good, let's go back to hair. What makes someone have a great hair style?"

I said it depended on a person's body type, age, facial structure, hair color/type, and overall sense of fashion. Then she asked me to list different types of styles—

bumps, crimps, perms, layers, colors, bangs—I went on and on… It reminded me of an IQ test I took in seventh grade where I had to list animals.

She asked me to explain my friends and my relationship with them. Once or twice she gave a little laugh and said she understood what I meant; she had a girlfriend like that. She asked me if I was the oldest sibling in the family. She has a little sister, a bit closer to her age than Jimmy is to me. She asked me if I had any heroes or heroines.

"Um, no, not really."

"Why not?"

My face got a little hot. "Um well it's not like I don't admire anyone. I mean I admire my mom. And my grandma is interesting."

"No one outside of your family?"

I seriously reflected on the question, "no."

"If you *did* have a hero or heroine outside of your family, what would they be like, what qualities would they possess?"

I kept peeking past Michelle at the window, "well I guess she would be highly respected."

"Ok that's a good trait," She patiently watched me again, "anything else?"

"She would be cool."

"Do you have a favorite book?" She gave me her strategic smile, "read outside of class though."

"I absolutely loved this story I read once. It's not a novel though."

"That's fine, what's the title?"

"*The Lottery.*"

"Oh, I haven't heard of that one before."

"You should definitely read it," but she had already

started typing. "Another one I liked, although I might have read it for school, is called, um, *Chrysanthemums*."

Michelle looked up from her screen and gave me a wide smile. I don't know how the fact escaped me before, but I finally noticed at that moment: *she had dimples*. "Oh that's a John Steinbeck." She paused for an instant, brightly smiling at her screen, "I wouldn't assume that they teach anything like that in public school. You probably read another short story by him for school."

I shrugged my shoulders.

"You have always gone to a public school right?"

"Yes"

"Eleanor, I'm not here to exploit you or anything like that."

Unsure I answered, "yeah."

"I am not, like, feigning an interest in you to sell you some stuff."

"Um, ok."

"Like your *Chrysanthemum* story, you won't find your flowers crushed on the side of the road. I promise you," a hint of personal pride pervaded her declaration, "what you tell me and show me will change the world around you."

I smiled, "alright."

Giving me a wide white smile, Michelle finished by saying, "Eleanor, I must say, you are an independent and articulate young woman, very mature for your age."

I must have blushed, "thanks."

"You are what we are searching for here at *Incantando*. Let me tell you what we would like you to do for us."

I was terribly happy.

She shifted in her seat and bent forward. "We would like for you to become a correspondent. You'll observe what's around you, your friends, classmates and peers, at school, at home, at sleepovers, hanging out, wherever. You are obviously observant already; we'd simply like you to write it down. What people are talking about, what they are wearing, what movies they like, what they drink, eat, laugh at, like anything really. The most important thing is to write what you feel is cool."

"Like a journal?"

"Yes, sort of," she inhaled and smiled, "it's better to consider it like a reporter or correspondent. It is unnecessary to write 'this is my opinion,' we understand who you are and where you are coming from. We have all that information about you." She smiled again, flashing her dimples, so subtle.

"When you notice something you find particularly cool, say so. Try to explain what you like about it, and don't worry what you think we like. We trust in your taste and style; we want to know what you like."

"So how often do you want these reports?"

"I'll give you a deadline. You'll have plenty of time, maybe once a month. I might text or email you about a particular clothing piece or item and the deadline will be shorter. So what do you think?"

"I'd love to do it."

"Great," suddenly she sat up straight and gave me a wide smile, her dimples so cute, "oh, and we have one of the latest cell phones for you."

"Cool."

"Stay here and I'll find out how many different colors we have left." She was gone for a minute or two and came back with three phones, all the same model, with cases in black, silver and red. I choose the red design.

"We are glad to have you with us Eleanor. For right now, the reports are what we'll have you do. We have other jobs if you're interested in working more, but we would rather utilize your talents in this position."

Trying to hide some of my confusion, I responded positively, "sure."

"And if you are punctual with your reports and the content is, like you know, quality, then we'll have a few rewards for you. Like letting you keep the smartphone or even a free shopping trip, although we would probably have Macy go with you to observe."

"Um, that's fine, I guess."

Michelle gave me a brochure for all the features of the phone. Michelle casually said, "if any of your friends ask you about the phone, be sure to tell them about some of these features."

The thing is basically a minicomputer—I know this dates the story, although I suspect people in the future will not even understand what I had in my pocket. It's not a phone, even calling it a computer is vague, and almost a lie, a massive lie we all tell ourselves. The thing is "connected" to "satellites" and the "internet." The unexplainable technologies construct reality, spells so powerful we believe that even to question their meanings or effects is mundane or silly. Michelle said that when humans could only travel overland by foot or horse, having horses greatly increased one's power and capabilities; and when she gave me the device I felt my capabilities increase ten-fold compared to the forces available to prior humans.

My mom sat in the waiting room as if she had never left me. She certainly seemed excited for me. Michelle never asked the questions my mom forecasted, but I didn't tell Mom that. As soon as we were in the safety of the car I wanted to talk to her about the glowing indigo room. However, once we arrived at the car she asked me about the interview and I unwisely showed her my phone. She flipped, "wow! They gave you that? Those aren't cheap Eleanor."

"I realize that."

In her typical fashion she chastened me, "be careful. Remember where you put it."

"Mom, I know."

"And are they paying for the service too?"

"Yep, everything, but they limit how much media I can download and how many minutes and text and that kind of stuff."

"I can't believe it, you got better perks than I do."

Surely she exaggerated. I desperately wanted to turn the conversation to the glowing room, what I heard, what it could mean. Frustratingly, my father called; I only heard part of the conversation.

"Hello"

. . .

"Yes, she got the job."

. . .

"Your father says congratulations."

. . .

"No." Her tone became agitated, "no, that's incorrect."

. . .

"No I didn't stick around."

. . .

"Why should I have stayed and had a coffee?"

. . .

"Yeah, ah-huh."

. . .

"Fine," Mom snapped the phone shut, remained quiet and a tense air filled the car. Occasionally, her body quivered. She took a few deep breaths.

"Eleanor, honey, your father and I have decided to separate for a bit."

"What do you mean?"

"We are spending some time apart."

The sound of the car grew loud in comparison to the silence in the car. All I could do was stare out the window at nothing in particular. Words failed to come to me.

"This has nothing to do with you or Jimmy, sweetheart."

"How long will you two be apart?"

"I don't know."

She could have been angry or sad. "Your father is staying at a hotel right now. You can call him if you want. I am sure he wants to talk with you."

What could I say? I wished I could have comforted her in some way.

"He would like to spend the weekend with you two; is that fine with you?"

"Alright."

After a long silence, I asked if they were getting a divorce.

Shortly, "I don't know."

We rode in silence to the house. Many of my friends' parents had divorced. I never thought much about my parents going through with it, yet it wasn't a surprise.

When I called my father, he had little more to add. He said the same things as my mom. Before we hung up he asked when was the last time I spoke with my girlfriends back home and suggested I call them. He never memorized their name. That's why he failed to mention Jamie or Ariel by name.

When I called Jamie, she gushed over my job; sadly I couldn't match her enthusiasm. She noticed, so I fudged a response and changed tack by mentioning the focus group. I desperately wanted to tell her about what I witnessed. After a long sigh, I tried to tell her, "Before my interview I went..." I had no idea what to say, "people are conspiring to infect the populace with a virus," wouldn't work, I would sound like a lunatic.

"Eleanor? Are you there?"

I would bring up the Agency office later, so I told Jamie how my parents were separating for a period. She asked if I wanted to talk about it, as if we could settle anything. Jamie's parents had been divorced since elementary school and everything seems to be going alright for her.

After another long pause, Jamie broke the silence, "this isn't too big of a shock, I mean, we saw this coming." I didn't respond right away, she was right.

"I guess so, Jamie."

"I mean, Eleanor, I've been over at your house for dinner with your parents."

"Yeah, and my dad is rarely home."

"Well, can you blame him, the table is totally cold? Your parents barely spoke to each other and when they did, it was like, nothing positive." Again, she was right. I had an epiphany eating dinner over at Ariel's house one night: my parents did not have a normal relationship. Her parents caringly touched each other, winked at each other, laughed together at inside jokes. I can't ever remember my parents doing that, maybe a quick coffee-breath kiss.

"Yeah, you're right. You've been over to Ariel's right?"

"Of course, I understand what you're getting at. So is everything alright with your parents? They're not like fighting and yelling or anything?"

"No, no. The other night they got into an argument." During another long pause I could picture Jamie sitting on her bed, knees together with one hand on her lap. She sat like that when she was tense.

"My dad is gone now. He is staying at a hotel and we might see him over the weekend." Jamie, who rarely made noises, sounded like a motor trying to start. She started to speak, abruptly stopped, and tried another word only to stop before uttering the entire first syllable. Finally she let out a long, "oh…"

After another pause she continued, "so how's your brother doing?"

"Jimmy's been crying since Mom told him. I doubt if he even knows why he is crying. He's cheered up a bit since Dad called."

"Well if you ever want to talk more about it, give me a call. Have you called Ariel yet?"

The thought of having to go through all these questions and formalities already bugged me. "Um, no. You could tell her and I could speak with her later."

"Ah, ok"

"It's getting kinda late and I'll call her later, I mean, it's not like my parents have divorced yet, or that like, it needs to be made a big deal or anything."

"I understand." But did she in fact? She was eight when her parents broke up. This last throw-away expression of sympathy annoyed me further and I didn't bring up what I heard at the Agency. An incredible opportunity lost, by the next time I spoke with Jamie, it would be too late to trust her.

CHAPTER SIX

DATE: _____

What I know <u>for sure</u> from the focus group and my job interview... At their office downtown, I clearly heard, "we are sending out a virus. Our target group is teenagers. First we go against this target, only then do we go against others. For the virus to succeed, we need an effective stealth campaign first." The voice came from a dark room emitting a blue light. I could not see into the room or hear the entire conversation because a man came by. Before I could clearly hear, I heard a few other words: "epidemic," "diffusion" which I thought might have been part of a propulsion system but now I understand it means "to spread." I also heard "sealed drinks" "carbonated drinks," "soda."

CHAPTER SEVEN

My mom dropped me off at school the next day. The sky completely blanketed by a low dark cloud, the air felt light. A cold wind billowed on a morning not caring to have a sunrise, sun or even rain, only endless grey. I appreciated barely being on time or late to school every day because awkward social situations could be avoided, along with the unpleasantly chilly weather. I got in a "hello" to a group of girls from English class before the bell rang and we compulsively headed for class.

Sitting in history class, I fingered my new phone on my lap, hidden in my coat. Michelle had sent a long email to give me instructions, find out if the service was running, and motivate me: "The pictures you take on your phone will change things that happened in the world." Michelle wanted my opinion and assured me other people would be listening to me and looking at my pictures through her and what I had told or shown her. Michelle also wanted a short report by the end of the week so that she could critique it.

I hardly noticed Mr. Sword as he droned on and on in

front of the chalkboard. I hadn't noticed anything special about the school, and I only had the six days to complete the report. I would have to search harder to find something I particularly liked. Looking around the class, nothing caught my eye, besides Mark of course. Something screams a calm confidence about Mark. He's quick with a smile.

"Again class, I hope I am not telling you the assignment too early in the morning, but that's the way it is. I already ran three-point-three miles before class; you have to do what you need to do to be prepared in the morning. I realize it's your first class of the day, but come on."

Some of the students shifted in their seats and frowned at Mr. Swords. These same students had even been softly whispering and gesturing at others. Mr. Swords continued composed.

"Alright, I will pick the groups for you. I have a handout that lays out the project as I have just explained."

Mr. Swords' voice boomed. Like a military instructor, he thrust out his arm pointing at people and calling out their last names, "Miller; Johnson; Bailey you're in a group." After calling the first person, he paused on the second and third names, searching the classroom. A captain making personnel decisions, he enjoyed himself.

Mark had yet to be picked. After Mr. Swords chose half the class, he bellowed "Callan! I want you with ... Moore and ... Stroud." That was Mark. How lucky.

Mr. Swords kept calling out the groups. Rob, as he liked to be called, and Mark were friends at school. They didn't hang out anywhere else though.

Rob's short, fiery, red hair capped his large figure. He's not too tall, just exceedingly round. His chest is barreled, but his stomach is so large that aspect of his physique goes unnoticed. His face is round, his green eyes and eye sockets even appeared especially round, almost cartoonish, a trait a caricaturist would drool over. Mark, of course, has a dream-like appearance with his bright sapphire eyes and his short slightly "moppy" dark brown hair. He's wearing a green shirt today, his muscular arms are tan.

"Good we got that done. By the end of class, only twenty minutes, I want at least two proposals for a topic and two ideas of some props for the presentation. Now remember, be creative. You could do a skit, bring in some pictures or drawings, but no food I am afraid, unless it's prepared, but then that wouldn't be colonial now would it. You'll have to meet outside of class to complete the project.

Beads of sweat became noticeable on Mr. Swords receding hairline. "As soon as you have two topics and two presentation ideas, come to me and I will write one on the board. Once the topic is up on the board no one else can use it, so work fast. If you need help with ideas for topics consider *Oliver Wisell*, the book you are supposed to have been reading or already read in English. Or you can ask me for advice. Now go to your groups!"

Chairs screeched, someone gave a loud "hey," a paper ball went flying across the class. Several students moved with their backpacks. Rob sat across from Mark, so I moved to them. As I approached the two I made sure to give Mark a smile.

Although Rob's voice was deep and pleasant, his tongue might have been too big, "…was totally a bad call. It should have had a video review."

Mark didn't return my smile. They went on about the

game the night before. Each end of Mark's shoe laces were tied into knots at the top of the shoe, as opposed to tied together in a bowtie. The sneakers had seen better days. They were covered in dirt and had a few scuff marks on them.

"Ah, see something interesting?"

"Oh," I could feel my face getting hot; I thought fast, "I like your shoes." He smiled, "thanks."

I thought he was happy because he knew that I liked him enough that I would lie about liking his dirty shoes.

"Yeah, they're pretty cool, huh."

Or maybe he was just a little dumb.

"My name is Eleanor, we haven't really met yet." The introduction came out a little pompous so I started to withdraw my extended hand, but it was too late. Mark stuck his hand out and we did a double take.

"Mark."

We eventually shook hands—a firm grip—his palms soft for a boy, yet large and potentially strong. My cheeks heated. I smoothly shook hands with Rob.

"Call me Rob." His hands were sticky.

Someone handed Mark the assignment papers, and Mark relayed them to me and Rob, who barely moved to reach for it. Rob comfortably filled his desk, only his mouth moved, "were you guys listening to everything?"

I faintly shook my head side to side. Mark buried his head in the paper, so I did too. We only had two weeks to give a ten minute presentation, no more or less, on one subject, comparing and contrasting the differences between now and 1770's America. The topic could be fashion, culture, food, transportation, etc…

After I finished reading I listened to the groups around

us. I'm not sure if Mark and Rob were still reading the assignment, thinking, or listening to other groups brainstorm for us. At some point a girl shrieked, "pets!"

"Nah, we need differences. Everyone probably had dogs and cats"

"Well, we have more selection nowww…"

"Oh, come on, that's totally boring."

Another girl in a high pitch tone said, "politics, they were forming a democracy, right?"

Mark finally broke our group's silence, "I suppose they could change the rules for video review in the last minute of the game."

"Yeah, that's what I'm sayin', too much is on the—"

"Get to work Moore!" Mr. Swords came towering over us. His hair curled a little extra because of the overcast weather. "If you fail to pick a topic by the end of class I'll assign you one." He then scrutinized the whole class and repeated the sentence even louder, as if everyone had a hearing problem. He quit harassing students and walked to his desk to grade papers.

I ventured a suggestion, "how about like people's goals. I mean, I realize everyone wanted to have their own country, but besides that. What did teenagers want to be when they grew up?"

Rob chimed in, "it's a good idea and all, but how many options did they have, nothing too cool."

We fell silent again, letting the others work for us.

Rob didn't move for sounding so excited, "we could talk about the illegal stuff people did."

"Dude, like what, murdering people? Mr. S. wants differences man."

I suggested, "we could talk about unacceptable things

people used to do."

"Good thinking Eleanor," Mark smiled at me as he spoke, "yeah, what would teenagers do that would piss off old grannies."

"Like *Quarters*."

"I doubt they would gamble with coins back then, they were worth so much more money dude."

"Yeah, but it's a difference from today."

We found a topic so I moved on, "if we find another gambling game then you two could play it as a part of our presentation."

"Awesome."

I stated the obvious, "we can use drawing or picture print-outs for about any topic."

"We need another topic though."

Rob sounded worked-up, yet he kept still, "what about what they did to them if they got caught!"

Delighted Mark added, "oh yeah, like tar and feathering,"

Rolling his round eyes and fat tongue, Rob lavished, "burnin'em alive!"

For some reason I thought of Michelle and some of the things that I heard at the Agency the day before. I kind of drifted from the conversation, examining the floor, when Rob said to me, "so what do you think Eleanor, we could have a witch trial and burn you alive as our prop?"

"Um, no."

"Oh come on, it would be good for your acting career, screaming and cursing the class as we pretend to light you on fire, it'd be sweet."

"Ah, no."

"Do either of you want to see Mr. S. about our topics?"

Rob slightly lowered his head and barely moved it side to side. Mark had his hands on the desk and his elbows high in the air ready to stand up, so I said no. With a wide smile, Mark approached Mr. S.'s desk across the classroom. Although the class buzzed with conversations, Mr. S.'s statements carried through all of them. He leaned forward as Mark spoke and then sat back in his chair.

"Do you even appreciate what was unacceptable in the 1770's? And then to compare it to nowadays, no, no, I don't want you giving your opinions on homosexuality nowadays."

Mark countered.

"Oh gambling, well, back then they had these fights, between a bull and several bulldogs. The bull would be on a chain," Mr. Swords gestured with his hands, "and people would bet on one of the animals. People also made side-bets when the bull used his horns to toss the dogs up in the air and people had to catch them with poles." The imaginary pole disappeared from Mr. Swords' hands. Despite the flourish, he dismissed the idea, "no, what else do you have?"

Mark spoke and Mr. S. answered, "torture, eh?"

"Oh, ok punishment, in your presentation you'd have to distinguish between the two." He adjusted his position in his seat. "Are you and Rob letting Eleanor give her opinion?" He lowered the volume of his voice yet it was still perceptible, "she might be shy." He glanced over at me watching him, nevertheless continued, unabashed, talking poorly about me.

"It's only her first week here. She might need some encouragement."

Mark spoke, and Mr. S. commented, "that's a good idea

too. Tell you what, go back over, vote for one of them and come back."

Mark returned and stayed standing. "He says we can't give a presentation on what pisses off grannies, and he enjoyed the topic Eleanor suggested. He said that we should…"

Rob spoke over him, "Well I vote for punishments."

I quickly added, "that sounds good to me too."

"Alright, I'll be right back."

Mark had to wait behind others. When he got to Mr. Swords the period ended. The instant the bell finished ringing Mr. S. began, "ok, those that are not on the board, shout out a topic for your group."

"Food."

"Fashion."

"Punishment."

Everyone packed up and left the classroom to head for their next class. As the day progressed along, several people invited me to join them for lunch. I said yes to the first and that I would love to have lunch with the others the next day or week.

The girl who invited me, Lilly, introduced me to everyone else at the table, five of us in all. I could tell these were a "popular" group. Others in the cafeteria watched us. A girl complimented me on my scarf, making me feel at ease. After some of the preliminary questions, where you from, what do you like to do, etc… I finally had a chance to eat my lunch.

A girl with long red hair started the conversation, "you can't even have like a normal conversation with Kelly. She always starts talking about her show dog." Lilly, sitting next to me, leaned over and quietly asked, "have you met

Kelly?"

Returning the tone in kind, "I don't believe so."

The redhead continued, "I'm mean, really, like that would ever happen." The redhead's pronunciation bubbled unevenly, vigilantly emphasizing and drawling out the vowels. Did she always speak in this style or was she was trying to ridicule the girl she was talking about? A few girls mechanically giggled at the redhead's last comment. Lilly leaned in again, "you'll know Kelly when you see her, she walks kinda funny."

All the girls had bagged lunches, lots of fruit and vegetables. They drank sealed bottles of juice mixes. I made mental notes of what they ate before they finished everything. I had to make my report.

"With her big nasty braces, she like could have been in that dog show movie as the kid of the couple with braces."

Without a hint of losing patience Lilly softly asked me, "have you seen, oh, I forgot."

"Lilly, quit, like, pestering Elly," the rhythmic pronunciation got at least one of the girls to giggle and I am sure the rest smiled.

"I'd prefer Eleanor."

The redhead beat a retreat, "oh, ok."

I turned to Lilly and said in a normal speaking tone, "you're talking about the dog show mockumentary with the lawyer couple with braces right?" Without waiting for a reply I turned and faced the table again, "she wouldn't be a good daughter for them though; it would have thrown off their freakish relationship with the dog."

A new girl chirped into the conversation, "well of course you don't; you haven't met Kelly yet."

Probably the most stylish girl added, "oh my gosh, I

know what movie you're talking about now, that is, like, so old."

I dropped the last subject. "So like what kind of dog does Kelly have?"

"It's a small dog."

"She probably feeds it cabbage too." Everyone laughed except me. Lilly giggled a bit and disregarded whispering to me.

"Like a terrier."

"No it's not a terrier."

"Then what is it Allison?"

"What is it that they like *do* at those shows anyways?"

"They walk their dog around, duh?"

"Yeah, showing that they can do it while chewing gum too." The whole table erupted in laughter. I smiled and sought what was so funny in the other's faces. Lilly quietly explained, "Have you met Jen yet?"

"Um, I met one the other day."

The girl across from us stared. The redhead elaborated, "she fell during lunch break last year in front of some people and she got up trying to make an excuse and said, 'I was just trying to chew some gum.'" Two of the girls giggled some more.

"Honestly, she's not that dumb, it was just a bad excuse."

"A horrible excuse…"

Talking over her, "no, that's not what she said Stacy; she said she was trying to get a piece of gum out." Lilly and the stylish girl still found it funny. So the redhead, Stacy, made the joke, although she wasn't even a witness.

"I'm sure Kelly doesn't do the showing of the dog."

Stacy said matter-of-factly, "that's just what I heard."

I started taking mental notes of each item of clothing the girls wore.

"They probably don't judge the person walking it."

"But how could anyone miss her, I mean could you picture her going up to the judges."

I said with a smile, "she'd probably blow a bubblegum bubble and get it all over her braces," I then leaned over the table a bit, flashed a square smile with my lower and upper white straight teeth, and shook my head a bit. I was attempting to make a joke. My braces were removed last year, but before then I once blew a bubble in front of class, a huge mistake.

One of the girls gave a giggle, but Stacy and the stylish blond remained silent, and the one across from me frowned. Lilly leaned into me again, "it's Jen that can't chew gum; Kelly walks funny."

"Are you girls ready to get out of here?"

After some nods of agreement, the girls began to leave. Lilly gave me a parting whisper, "oh I got it now, Kelly has braces and the gum would be stuck." I smiled and got my stuff together too but remained seated. I thanked them for a nice lunch and mumbled about needing to do something. Once they left I got out my notebook.

I jotted notes to myself about what everyone wore and ate. After about five minutes, I had an awkward feeling, perhaps from a shadow reflecting on the table. I adjusted my head to make out the form. I felt someone behind me, watching. When I turned, no one was there, only Stacy with her long red hair, not far from me, leaving the cafeteria. Much later I concluded that this incident probably ended my chances at genuine relationships with the popular girls at school.

• • •

That night I sat on our old couch in the new living room with one of those standard TV-static covered journals. Jimmy played on the computer. On the cover, in the middle of squiggling white marks, I left blank the white box with the word "title." At the top of the first page I wrote:

What you say and show me will change the world around you.

My notes included many details; only during that year would it be completely understood. I wrote about different items of clothing: colors, sizes, designs, combinations, series, extensions of styles, gaps between styles, ways of wearing, percentages, and cliques. I wrote what people wore according to their body: size, shape, height, gender, and ethnicity. I wrote what I liked, what I didn't like and why.

At some point Jimmy let out a cry, "whoa, hey check it out Elly, I got a free soda for my birthday!"

"But it's not your birthday for another couple of months…"

He squealed over my voice, "and the soda's blue!" An indigo advertisement flashed on the top of the screen above his avatar's statistics. I hadn't heard of a blue soda before. I wrote my thoughts on the notepad until late in the night.

• • •

With an exception of a curious incident, the next day rattled on much like the one before. I went to classes, had lunch with a different group of girls, and when I got a chance, I jotted some notes about what I observed and heard. By afternoon, I had trouble focusing on class, so much seemed to be going on. After twice losing the thread of lecture, an unaccustomed experience for me, I needed to take a break to clear my head. I got excused to use the restroom which I unwisely used as a destination.

Low overcast clouds formed a dark ceiling as I crossed the courtyard. Occasional gusts of wind jerked silvery trash on the concrete, producing the sound of a rake. I had no problem finding a restroom, although I walked much further than necessary. Inside, I washed my face attempting to remove the darkening rings under my eyes. On the way back, I got turned around, I may have exited and went the opposite direction. I went to the courtyard to get my bearings. The wind seemed to have stopped. Once I reached the center, I turned completely around, facing where I came from and saw a petite freshman girl, framed by the prison-like gateway, staring at me. She wore double denim and had light brown hair, but a neon blue bottle of soda in her hand dominated her appearance and gave a strange justification for existing outside during class hours, amongst iron gates, staring at an older peer. She started speaking to me, too low and too far to hear, yet her words floated across the trash laden courtyard as incomprehensible Latin. No doubt she spoke to me, her eyes never shifted from mine. She never blinked. She stopped, quickly blew a pink bubble with gum and when she snapped it up with her teeth, a wind blew in her hair.

She recommended the low Latin vowels and the wind gust increased in intensity carrying more and more of her hairs above her head, despite the complete stillness of air around me. The tone of her incantations became spiteful. Her eyes narrowed while her hair tangled above her head like mating snakes. I broke off eye contact and glanced around at all the trash on the stained concrete around me—none of it moved because there was no wind. She abruptly stopped, the wind started to die and she took a long glug of her blue soda. I ran back to class, I had seen enough.

Obviously, the break did nothing to help my classroom attention. The remainder of the school day drifted by in a blur. That night Ariel called. I had to go through some of the "pleasantries" about my parent's separation. Ariel had little to add; her parents had a great relationship.

"Hey, this will cheer you up, go to Ylime's website. Wait until you see what that princess posted." A high school girl from the same suburb as me created an online persona called Ylime. Her website had a videocast of her talking about the most mundane, stupid stuff. Habitually, she provided a decent laugh, as in laughing *at* her not *with* her. She had put a video application for reality TV programs. Not a specific program, any reality show, the title of the webcast was "Application for Reality TV."

"I'll have to watch it later." The first frame of the video contained Ylime in a skinny tank top. Despite being underage, she revealed a lot of skin. Her skimpy attire was a running joke: she failed to recognize her real audience. Of course, in retrospect, she knew it all too well...

Finally I got to some more pressing issues, my new job. I told her about the job, except for the interview, I wanted to deliberate over it more. Ariel couldn't be more surprised that I got actually got paid to do what they wanted me to do.

"Wow, you like won a small lottery!"

"I guess so."

"That kinda sounds like what Amy did."

"Oh, Amy who?"

"Kruss. We used to play softball together, but she went to another school."

"What did she do?"

"She had these sleepovers where she'd get a bunch of cool stuff. She'd invite over some friends and she'd have this big box with all kinds of stuff in it."

"Like what?"

"Hair bows, sleep masks, clothing, and all kinds of stuff. The company had assignments or games for us. Like, we'd vote on our most favorite item. Occasionally we'd watch a music video or a movie. I guess I was about eleven or twelve."

"So how's that like what I told you?"

"Oh, well I found out later the party's purpose was marketing research. The name of the agency was like the intelligence agency or whatever."

"Is she still doing it?"

"No, well maybe she still does it, but she hasn't invited me."

"Did you ever try any, like, soda at these sleepovers?"

"No, we didn't have any food. Well, actually we did have food and drinks, but I don't think we ever had anything new, that we, like, voted on or played with or whatever."

While I digested everything she said, Ariel said

something very strange, in a voice as if she was right next to me. "How come you are asking Eleanor?"

I paused, confused about her voice. I tried to listen to her breathing, but only silence carried over the line. Finally, I ventured a reply, "um, I'm just curious?"

"How come you are curious Eleanor?"

Again, she sounded as if she was in the room with me.

"Just forget about it."

At that moment, I decided not to bring up the soda drinking girl who spoke Latin in the wind. Nonchalantly Ariel went back to normal, "hey it's getting pretty late... it's almost midnight."

"Oh, I wanted to ask you about Darcy's brother," the brother that went to the mental hospital.

"I don't know too much about that."

"I know I just wanted...," I wasn't sure what to say, "what is he up to?"

"Can we talk about it more tomorrow?"

"Sure."

"Love you sweetie."

"Love ya."

Once I hung up with Ariel I brought up Ylime's website. She had a section entitled "gifts" where her admires can find out what stuff to ship to her P.O. Box. I recall reading a product I hadn't heard of before. She wanted "a twelve pack of Tru Blue," and posted a picture of an ad of Tru Blue soda with the slogan: "Is it you?" The caption for the photo, Ylime's reply, "hell yes! I fell asleep as soon as I lay down, another late night.

CHAPTER EIGHT

The next day's afternoon, I had English with Mark. The due date for our project bothered me, especially since I would be with my father over the weekend. Discussing the project would be a good excuse to talk with him. Most of the class I thought about how our conversation the previous morning could have been so much better. As class ended, I packed my stuff and was preparing what to say, when I heard his voice, "hey Eleanor."

"Oh hey,"

"So I spoke with some of the guys and Mr. Swords is totally screwing us."

"How so?"

"In previous years he gave students another week! We only have one weekend to get the project done."

"Yeah, I am like sorta busy this weekend."

"Busy huh?"

"Yeah, with some stuff, I doubt I would be able to meet"

"I can't believe he shortened the time for the

assignment."

"Maybe I could talk with him before class, find out if he'll give us another due date or more in-class time."

"Good idea. I'd like more class time. What about after school today? Rob said we could go to his place. I have practice at four though."

"Sounds good, let me call my mom first, I have a little brother that I have to pick up from a day care."

"Alright, how you gonna…?"

Standing up I leaned towards Mark, "I have a phone, for emergencies."

"Cool, yeah Rob does too. He already called his mom about us coming over."

"What's Rob's mom's number?"

"I don't know, hey, let's meet out front by the flagpole after school. If you can't come I'm sure Rob and I can figure some stuff out."

"I'll make it." I could call my mom from school and explain the situation.

Phones are not allowed at my new school, or old one. I'm supposed to check the messages while in the bathroom every day. I check it, just somewhere else. Last year when I got caught, my parents grounded me for a week.

Once the last bell rang, the sky had darkened and tiny rain drops silently fell outside. Rob and Mark were not at the flagpole, so I searched nearby cover. As soon as I found them Rob led us to his mom's car. She certainly passed as Rob's mother, short red hair, round shaped body, eyes, nose, and face. I wondered what Rob's father looked like? Rob could have been inherited all his genes from his mother, they were so similar.

Ms. Moore asked me inane questions all the way to her house. Despite the short trip, I had no idea where we were. I didn't even get to check the surrounding area once the car stopped since the rain picked up and all of us ran into the house. Well, Ms. Moore walked; she is heavy set.

Rob pointed to the computer in the living room but went straight to the fridge in the kitchen. The whole space was open.

"Start it up, there's no password. Would you guys like anything to eat or drink?"

"Oh, we should stick with juice, honey."

"Mommm…"

"What kind of juice do you have Rob?

"Orange and cran-apple."

Everyone had cran-apple. We placed two kitchen chairs around the leather computer chair. Jackie, as Ms. Moore wanted to be called, set about doing some work in the kitchen.

"Get those granola bars…, they have lots of vitamins in them."

Already eating, Rob brought over a handful of chewy granola bars. Sticky and varying in consistency with chewy chocolate or marshmallows, they grossed me out, but I devoured a bar and thanked Jackie and Rob.

Mark brought up YouTube and searched "colonial punishments."

"Whoa, check it out; we should totally do that in class."

Rob came over to watch. "Ha! That would be pretty good."

"I guess you could bring a change of clothes, but you'd still probably smell like syrup all day."

Rob couldn't care less, "I'll do it. We could tear open a

pillow for the feathers."

The video bounced around from an unsteady cameraman, little action occurred, just lots of giggling off camera, not exactly the best use of our time. At least we got one of the performances. I waited for the boys to finish reading the comments and tire of the video.

"I'll do the witch burning. In class I was just..."

Jackie had turned on the trash-compactor in the kitchen.

"Alright cool."

We waited for the trash-compactor to finish. "Yeah, I thought about it some more, instead of screaming at the class, I could put a spell on them."

"Sweet, good thinking."

"And I could act all drunk while you tar and feather me."

"Is that why they tarred people though?"

"Hey, let's do a video, we could do all the punishments, whipping, hanging, burning and whatever else."

Mark dismissed the idea, "dude, its only two-hundred points and we only get fifty for the props." He grabbed a pen and paper and quickly explained to us what percent the project had for the whole course. When Rob mentioned it would be different for me because I missed some school, Mark knew from memory how many points had already been available and worked out my percentages.

"What do you think Eleanor?"

"You're quick at..."

The garbage disposal in the sink came on. "No I mean..."

Mark had to shout over the noise, "oh, we should get a good enough grade having two skits, unless you two really want to make some videos."

Rob sunk back into his seat and took out another chewy granola bar, "yeah, ok, so what else, I, arumunchuch, was imagining, arumunch, we'd cover two unique colonial punishments along with imprisonment then and now: Eleanor gives the introduction and conclusion because those will include modern day punishments; I'll get tarred by Eleanor, Mark talks about that; I'll talk about witch burning while you two act that out." He went on eating while he stood up and headed to the fridge. Jackie had left the room, but noises still came from the house.

The heater kicked on. Mark searched the internet for other punishments. "Oh, I found a list here ... the stocks, whipping posts, branding,"

At that point I realized—I stood in the exact same layout as my new house—the door entrance way, the "open concept" living room and kitchen.

"...tarring and feathering was used for tax collectors loyal to the British government..."

The ceiling, the hallway, I could be in my house's layout. The refrigerator started to vibrate since Rob had been searching through it. "Whoa! Sweet!"

"I'll research why they burnt witches and send it to you Rob."

"Guys, check it out guys, a new soda!"

Rob came back with three indigo soda cans in his hand, they felt vaguely familiar. He put two on the desk, cracked the can open and took a big swig. Mark grabbed one; I turned my can to face me with its name: Tru Blue. Suddenly I had an intense yet vague recollection, like an episode from a dream. I blurted out, "Mark don't drink that!"

He blankly stared at me. A can of Tru Blue gripped in his hand.

Serious and softly I added, "I wouldn't drink that."

Rob had finished half his soda by then, let out a belch and asked, "Why not?"

"Cause…"

"What's wrong?" He inspected the soda and spun the can to read the label. Much more normal sounding I said, "It's just that, you said you had practice at four, right?" the doorbell rang, "Well you don't want that right before practice."

Rob went for the door and Mark read the time on the computer, "whoa, where's your Mom dude, I'll be late." He set the soda on the desk and got up. Rob called his mom and she immediately appeared from around the corner, "who's at the door Rob?"

In a quieter voice she asked, "am I dropping you off at the elementary school Eleanor?"

"Huh, oh yeah."

"Sorry I didn't notice the hour, Mark, I'm ready, let's go."

The rain had slowed. Rob came with us too, he brought his soda. We rode in an awkward silence. When Mark hopped out at the gymnasium he only said "thanks" to Jackie. From the front seat, without turning back to examine me, Rob inquisitively asked, "ah, Eleanor, is like everything ok?"

"What, huh, yeah, it's just, your house has the exact floor plan as our new house."

Jackie chuckled in the driver's seat. Rob kept silent. "Oh, you must live in the same subdivision as us. The builders designed fifteen different houses." She chuckled more, a blubbery hacking sound which reminded me to make sure I had my seatbelt on. It sounded like she had a bizarre medical condition. To clear her throat, she took a gulp of Tru Blue. Rob laughed similar to his mom, but slightly more normal sounding. He wasn't laughing though.

"I'll give you a ride to your place. The rain isn't letting up."

"Thanks."

I half expected Rob to offer my little brother a soda when he got into the SUV. Instead we rode in silence except for my directions; I guess Jackie used all her questions on me. When we arrived at the house, I used the rain as an excuse to run to the door.

I suppose James didn't notice the tension in the car. He seemed like his normal self. "Guess what Eleanor, I made a friend today. He invited me to his birthday party on Sunday!"

"That's great Jimmy, I have some work to do though."

"Isn't that cool? A birthday party."

"We're hanging out with Dad over the weekend."

"Yeah I know, hey I want to use the internet."

"James, I said that I have some stuff to do. You always use the computer when we get home."

"Gee, you don't have to get angry with me."

He went to his room. I went to Ylime's website, started her videocast, and opened another tab for her wish-list. In her sweet ditsy accent she rambled on about being a good reality TV participant. I stopped the video. In the corner of the screen, a can of Tru Blue blinked fluorescent indigo.

I searched the internet: *Incantando's* website, Tru Blue,

Michelle Mayer, virus. I searched these terms in the news, forums, and in connection with "conspiracy," "government cover-up," "witches" and "terrorist." Tru Blue was a new soda which had plastered their slogan across the internet: "Is it you?" There was nothing unusual.

I searched until my mom got home. Rapidly closing everything, I grabbed some paper and scribbled on it when she came in. When my mom opened the door, darkness hid the outside.

Everyone remained quiet through dinner. Jimmy talked about his new friend he made at the afterschool center. Mom said nothing about our father.

I had trouble sleeping that night. The next day would be Friday and I would be with my dad for the first time since he drank the creamer. I kept reflecting about the definition of a virus.

CHAPTER NINE

DATE: _____

A "virus" is an organism that needs a host to reproduce. Because it cannot replicate by itself, scientists don't consider it to be living. From my searches, both Michelle, Macy, and _Incantando_ ("Enchanting" in Italian) do not appear to have any connections with terrorist, our government (or any government), or secret societies. The Agency, headquartered in New York, has several other offices.

<u>Incantando</u> is a boutique research and marketing firm. I feel I saw Tru Blue before the interview at the Agency. I might have seen it reflected from the flat-screen.

CHAPTER TEN

The next morning I made sure that my mom got me to school early. I wanted to talk with Mr. Swords about our in-class time for the project, although we got a lot done in thirty minutes yesterday. The morning was clear, and teeth hurting cold if I yawned.

I hesitated at the door into history and knocked first. Amazingly clear, I heard, "come in."

"Hello Mr. Swords, I have a question about our presentation."

"Ah yes, sit down, I thought you would."

I sat down in the chair directly across the desk from him. His size was bigger than in front of the class, even though he was sitting down. Perhaps he was an athlete in college.

"I doubt anyone has ever done a presentation on colonial punishments. I suppose you're wondering about how to organize the topic?"

"Well…" I started to speak, but gave up as he talked over me, "you need a framework. Let me put it this way.

Every year a group will chose food—they cover breakfast, lunch and dinner. Yet you should think of other questions to answer. Why do we eat? Every now and then someone realizes the human relationship aspect. In the colonial era people were poor and sharing food was a way of solidifying connections among non-blood relations; whereas, nowadays sharing a meal with family and friends is not as intense." I wanted to tell him to try eating in the cafeteria.

His head tilted ever so slightly, back and forth as he spoke. I noticed the tilting because sometimes his glasses caught the light and flashed white, hiding his blue eyes. "What I am trying to tell you is if you say, 'food is energy,' or 'punishment is for wrong-doing,' you are not doing well. Again for presentations on food a good group covers: *how* we ate, *where* we ate, *what* we ate, and *who* ate what, as well as the answer to those questions in modern America." I happened to know that my ancestors were not in America before the Revolution.

"Ok, thanks, we'll keep that in mind. We have already done some organization and that's not why I…"

He interrupted, "what have you all came up with so far?"

"We decided to cover three punishments, one each: tarring and feathering, witch burning, and imprisonment. We'll act out the two colonial punishments, while the other talks about what crimes led to which punishment, how the punishment took place, where it typically happens, and who all these people were." I made some of this up because Mr. Swords upset me a bit.

"Mmm, was it Rob that came up with that organization?"

"No, we all did." Not really a lie since I only this minute made up some of that stuff. I could detect some disbelief in his mouth, his eyes hidden behind a flash of light. "You think I'm stupid, don't you!? You put me with Rob and Mark who are both *obviously* smart."

Mr. Swords leaned back in his seat more, maybe he was even blushing, "no, no I don't have access to any of your test scores or your grades and performance reviews from your old school. Which does remind me," he leaned forward again, his glasses filled with light reflecting at me, "you have to be more detailed with modern imprisonment, because we only have one punishment, and you should consider if people had as many records and documents about them in the colonial period as they have now."

The conversation was not going the way I wanted and I bent my head down to regard my hands folded in my lap. In an unusually quiet voice, Mr. S. asked, "is it you?"

My eyes shot up. Mr. S. was not looking at me as he reached for his coffee when the bell rang. Once he lifted the cup off his desk, I could see three empty creamers. The ringing was incredibly loud, but he didn't flinch; his glasses had permanently caught the light. When the bell stopped ringing, he started instantaneously, "now tell me, what is the reason you wanted to talk to me?"

The door opened and a few students came in. "I... I just wanted to say, that um, I don't think we have enough time outside of school to put everything together and I was wondering if we could have some class time."

"*More* class time?"

"Um, you didn't say we'd have any."

"Oh, I must have forgotten to tell your class. Thanks for reminding me. I will this morning."

More students had been coming in. I went to my seat. Mark entered, head-up, but he walked to his seat looking down. Rob was absent. Mr. Swords announced we would have in-class time for the presentations, but not this day. As soon as the bell rang, Mark quickly left, never looking towards me. In English class, he at least glanced at me, although I had the sense he wanted to avoid me.

I was late to the last class of the day. And once again I witnessed classmates drinking the blue soda. This time I came around a corner and, at a distance, saw three girls at the same iron gateway as the petite spell-caster. They spoke to no one in particular or perhaps each other without the common courtesy of looking at each other. A gentle gust blew on the three as they awkwardly posed, blue drinks in hand. I attempted to discern the words or meaning, but I could only distinguish a pattern of intonations. One quietly soloed and another broke into a quick chirp only a few Latin syllables before the first stopped. The third returned to the low mumblings. The wind blew the hardest on the current speaker. Once again no trash blew in the courtyard. I got the sense they would see me at any moment so I double backed and arrived even later to class.

By the end of the school day it was not much warmer. My brother and I shivered all the way home. I wanted to do some more research, so James went into his room again. My father called.

"Eleanor, I'm looking forward to seeing you this evening. I should swing by at about six thirty instead of six, and we'll get some pizza ok?"

"Sounds good Dad."

"I'm also calling about Sunday. I need to go into work

sweetie. I know we planned to spend the weekend together but it's been incredibly busy."

I was relieved. "That's ok, Dad, I know."

"Let James know. I already spoke with your mom."

I continued reading about carbonated drinks and milk when less than ten minutes later the phone rang again. Mom wanted to know if I had spoken with Dad and sounded disappointed, calling his cancelation, "typical."

"Well, your brother will get to go to this birthday party. What do you say we go shopping?"

"Sure."

"It will be just like old times. We haven't really gone shopping together since we moved. I've already checked out a few new places. I'll tell you about it when you get home Saturday evening." Her voice had quickly changed to excitement.

"You should get a change of clothes packed to stay at the hotel with your father. He's taking you two to the city zoo and the museum."

"Alright, I'll tell James."

"Ok, take care sweetie, I won't see you before your father arrives. I need to get some things done at the office before the weekend."

James seemed energized about the weekend plans. He even got off the couch, and sensing he had nothing to do off the couch, he got something to eat and returned. Not more than ten minutes from my mom's call, the phone rang yet again—Macy from the Agency.

"So the reason I am calling is to see if you would mind if I came shopping with you."

I was silent for a beat.

"What?"

"I'd like to come with you shopping for clothes, accessories, makeup, shoes, just about anything you'd like really. We would even give you some money to spend."

I tried to compute the relationships between everyone.

"Eleanor, are you there?"

"Yes, um, well my mom and I are going shopping this weekend."

"Yes I know I spoke with your Mom and Dad already."

I remember standing in the kitchen with the phone to my ear.

"Hello Eleanor, I think we have a bad connection."

"Yes."

"So do you want to go?"

"Sure."

"Great, I'll call your mom back and let her know. I wasn't sure about my scheduling earlier."

"Sure, anything you want me to do?"

"No, just shop, I'll talk to you more about it in person. We'll meet sometime Sunday morning."

"Sounds great."

"Have you started working on your report?"

"Yes."

"How far are you along? Do you have something typed?"

"Yes, it's about four pages, double-spaced."

"Go ahead and send it in then so we could give you any pointers if there is anything we'd like you to change." She didn't seem at all impressed by the length.

"Sure."

"Good, goodbye Eleanor."

I slowly put the phone back into its charger. I hopped on the computer, reread what I wrote and made sure it contained no mistakes and sent it off. After hastily getting ready for Saturday, I sat on my bed thinking.

Suddenly I heard a quick series of obtrusively loud knocks from the front door and immediately, I wondered if I locked the door behind me earlier. The sound of the door opening confirmed my forgetfulness and someone angrily entered the house. Then I heard a deep voice from inside the house, "hey kids, you ready to go." As I opened the door and started to walk slowly down the hallway I could hear the last few running steps of Jimmy as he reached my father. Jimmy rambled on and on about his week and his new friend and the birthday party.

"Whoa, slow down there kiddo."

He picked Jimmy up. When he saw me he came up to me to give me a hug. I couldn't remember the last time he hugged me before then. His body felt foreign, his smell different, his grip too strong. If he wanted to force feed me Tru Blue, it would not be any problem for him.

"Ok, you guys ready for some pizza?"

"Yeah!"

As we started walking out of house my father asked, without even looking at me, "how you doing, Eleanor?"

"Um, good I guess."

He was at his four-door sedan now and still not looking at me, "How's school?"

"Good, I…"

He spoke over me, "Could you lock the door, Eleanor?"

Using an extra key my mother gave me a few days ago, I went to the front door of my house and locked it. The simple act seemed to take forever and the air had a knowing pressure, my father must know that I know he no longer has a key to the house. When I came back to the car Jimmy sat in the front seat, "I called shotgun!" I got in the car behind Jimmy and we set our bags on the middle seat. I had no idea where we were going. Jimmy rambled on and my dad kept him going by asking more questions. My father unceremoniously said that he had a surprise for James. We got onto a freeway. Everything was completely dark. I saw signs that we were going towards the city.

"Ok, ok James," in a voice a little bit louder, "what do you two want on your pizza?"

"Sausage and cheese!"

"The ads on TV say that we can get two medium sized pizzas Eleanor."

"Um, maybe Hawaiian."

"I thought that we would stay in tonight instead of going out. Maybe talk a bit. We could also order a pay-per-view movie on the TV."

He started to order the pizza. I could hear the man on the other line asking questions. When he asked for an address, my father just gave him his cell phone number and the man on the other line read an address back to my father, but I couldn't make it out, just a part of a larger number, "84-."

"That's correct. Ok thanks," he hung up his cell.

After a few more exits, he got off on Drewski Ave. We took two turns and pulled into a hotel on Golden Heights Avenue. The name of the hotel was also "Golden Heights." When I searched it online I found that it's a popular chain of hotels; they merely changed their identity to the name of the street to appear local. At the time though, I had no idea where we were, just some random hotel.

My stomach started to cramp up really bad as we hit a bump pulling off the street. I remember thinking that it was so soon, a waxing quarter moon already? The weather had been so cloudy for the past week. I tried to look up into the night sky, but we pulled into a building, the parking lot was in the basement. Yellow lights shone on a concrete floor and walls.

"Your mother didn't want you two to come here tonight, she thought maybe you two would feel uncomfortable. But try to think of it as a vacation. Tomorrow we're going to the zoo and a museum we haven't been to before."

Neither Jimmy nor I said anything; we made our way to the elevators. Inside the elevator another couple joined us. Nobody said anything. We got off on the fifth floor; there were six floors in all. As soon as my dad opened the hotel room, my bother said he was thirsty and I said I needed to use the bathroom.

The bathroom was very sterile. Everything was wrapped up, the soap, toilet paper, cups. A faint flora scent seemed to cling to the room; no amount of soap could get rid of the smell. The door shut with a metallic latch sound and the room had a muffled silent room quality. I could no longer hear my brother's and father's conversation. When I was done, I took my time washing my hands and studied myself in the mirror, the dark rings below my eyes were worse, as if I didn't go to sleep the night before.

Glancing down as I opened the door, my dad was right in front of me standing sideways. He's probably six foot high, not muscular, but he could certainly overpower me. Some dark stubs protruded along his chin, something rather primal, a shadow of facial hair. He was paying for the pizza.

I followed behind him to a small table in the back corner of the room where my brother sat. As my Father negotiated himself around the small room and put the pizzas on the table, I saw the Tru Blue in my brother's hand.

"Hey Eleanor, check out the surprise Daddy got for me!" I was speechless. "I asked him and he found it!"

I slowly sat down facing the window curtains with my father and brother to my sides. A Tru Blue was sweating like an advertisement on the table in front of me, along with a paper towel. Both of them picked up a slice and started eating. I merely sat there.

"Here honey let me get you some slices."

He put a slice of Hawaiian pizza on my paper towel.

"Would you like me to get this for you?" He gestured to open my Tru Blue with his one clean hand.

"No, I, I don't want it."

"Would you like a different soda?"

"Um…"

Jimmy tilted his head to the side, screwed his eyes up at me, and asked, "is it you?"

I must have made a face because Jimmy chortled at me. My father hadn't seen the interaction. "It's really good though, you haven't tried it yet, huh? I think you'll like it. Isn't it good James?"

"It's the best! I love Blue."

"No, it's just that it has too much sugar."

My father turned the can in his wrist, "well, yeah I guess that's a lot, but it's pizza."

"Yeah, you can't have pizza without soda dummy."

"James!" He gave James a reprimanding glare. "There is

a vending machine down the hall with some juice in it I think."

"No, I think water is perfectly fine." I stood up and got some lukewarm, nasty hotel tasting water and sat back down.

"You're not on a diet or anything honey?"

"Oh, no."

"Ok, because you certainly don't need to be. You still want pizza right?"

I took that as a cue to start eating. My father actually smiled when I started eating. He smiled every time he gave me a new piece that night. After everyone had a slice my father started speaking again.

"You've been really quiet Eleanor." His eyes dropped down at his pizza, "how's school going? I am sure that you have been making friends."

"Yeah, I guess so. It's kinda strange because everyone knows everyone else and I don't know what people are talking about most of the time."

"Hmm, inside jokes and everything, yeah, I get that at work too." I hadn't really been thinking about my father's work. I suppose I simply pictured him staying in the hotel room drinking creamers, or meeting with Michelle and Macy.

"How's work been Dad?"

"Oh, it's coming along you know. I got a lot more responsibility, and right now I am focusing on getting up to speed. Thanks for asking."

The tips of my cheeks felt hot for a moment. We ate some more. At some point, Dad must have put on the TV to a classical music station. A symphony of violins and horns was flaring up and drowning down.

"Do you have any interesting teachers at this new school?"

Mr. S. came to mind. "Not really."

"We do have this group presentation due next week that's a bit interesting."

"Oh, a presentation... how many are in the group? Are you using any visuals?"

"There are three of us and we are doing colonial punishments. We are supposed to contrast them with modern-day punishments. We decided to perform a skit."

"Ah, and how do you plan on using the skit to communicate the subject matter?"

"Well, the props are a percentage of the grade, and Mr. Swords is grading them on creativity and accuracy in portrayal."

"Eleanor, I give or listen to presentations every week at work. Just because a visual or a prop is accurate doesn't mean that it is being used in a way that communicates information. And creativity doesn't help anything if it only attracts attention but still confuses people. Props are to facilitate what you want to communicate. I don't know about your teacher, but I am sure you'll do a good job on the skit. So what's the skit?"

"Well, I'm going to pour syrup and throw feathers at Rob while Mark talks about it. And then Rob will present while Mark acts as a guard to tie me up to burn as a witch. We haven't thought about what we are going to say yet, but I will probably put some kind of curse on everyone."

"Eleanor, what are you trying to communicate with the skit?"

"Ah," my words came out choppy, "what, it, was, like, to be punished in colonial America, I guess."

"Ok, so do you see any problems with your tar-and-feathering skit?"

"Um, Dad, we can't, like, bring real tar into the classroom, I mean, come on."

"I don't know too much about colonial history, but I don't think one person feathered someone who had tar thrown on them."

"Ah, yeah, I guess it was more than one person."

"Maybe I'm wrong, but wasn't it a mob, right?"

"Yeah, I think so, that's not my topic to present though."

"Eleanor, you have to work as a team, and if you're acting, you should put in some effort to get into character."

"That isn't fair; that's doing Rob's work for him."

"Eleanor, you're very likely to be working in teams your entire life, and that attitude will not get you far. True, everyone needs to be accountable, but ultimately anyone who amounts to anything must take responsibility for all."

Something was definitely different with my dad. I said sheepishly, "ok."

"When you get older you'll understand. You'll see various mechanisms to ensure accountability in group projects, making sure everyone is measured, and rewarded for their quality and efficiency. I am sure your teacher will notice the work you put in. They are well trained nowadays."

Jimmy interrupted for another slice, "Dad can you get me another piece, please?" He was at the age where kids simply ignored adults, instead of listening to the confusing babble. Dad handed Jimmy another slice.

For the first time that night, or perhaps over the

weekend, my dad finally looked searchingly into my face, like he used to do. "Now, about witch burning..." He glanced at the window curtains, pulled them shut and then back at me, "You don't really believe in witches right?"

I hesitated, "no."

"I don't know exactly who it was that *they* used to burn," his emphasis was quick and subtle, "but I did read something recently. You know, historically women have not been that independent; having their own jobs and everything, and single independent women would be burned at the stake if they were a little weird. Some people suggest independence is the reason for the fifty percent divorce rate."

"What do you mean?"

"Oh, nothing."

"Is that what happened to you and Mom?"

"No, no. This has nothing to do with your mother being financially independent. That's a good thing, believe you me."

"Oh, ok."

"And they certainly wouldn't have tried her as a witch; they only did that to non-conformist."

Jimmy, who probably had less of a clue than me, asked, "may I have another soda Daddy?"

"Sure, why not?"

I said to Jimmy, "you know you're not supposed to have more than one soda a day Jimmy."

"Oh your sister's right James. Tell you what, how about we just split one."

James brought back a cup with his new soda from the mini-fridge. Once James had a full cup, he jumped out of the seat again, "what movie are we going to watch?" Like most spastic kids, his limbs seemed to move without thought or control sometimes. He reached for his cup and knocked it over.

"Oh no, I'm sorry. Oh no," he sounded deeply disturbed.

"Don't worry about it son, it's just one spilled cup. No need to cry over one spilled cup. Here, have mine. I will get another one."

My father opened another Tru Blue and as if the crack was a thought going off in his head, he announced, "oh, I forgot, we have a great view of the city from here. Eleanor, open the window shades." My father walked to the door of the room and just as I found the cord and started opening the window shades, he flipped the lights off.

The lights of the city were spectacular. We were rather close, so close that I am sure we couldn't see all the buildings behind some of the bigger ones. "Which one is yours Daddy?"

"Oh you can't see it from here," he came walking over in the dark, "I'll take you kids there next weekend if you'd like."

"Ok."

"You like all the lights, Jimmy?"

"Yeah, it's cool."

"It's Friday night… the janitors stay later to do a better cleaning, that's why there are so many lights."

This definitely wasn't the city I knew or at least had been to before. Yet how well did I know our last city? And how different could they really be? Suddenly the lights came back on and Jimmy and I saw a reflection of ourselves in the window, the city barely perceptible beyond us. Neither of us moved, we simply stared at each other, examining and comparing our features as we did a few years ago, seeing if the city lights changed anything.

We watched some superhero movie and then went to sleep. Jimmy and Dad shared one bed and I got the other. My father didn't offer me any more Tru Blue or any sealed drink.

That night I dreamt of glasses of water. A whole world filled with glasses of water. The glasses varied in shape and size; the water levels varied from the brink to none. At first, I sat on the couch, at our old home, surrounded by dozens of glasses of water in the living room. Some of the glasses rested on the couch, many others on the coffee table, some scattered about the floor. Then I sat in a desk at my new school, a few glasses of water laid here and there, at least one on most people's desk, a few canning jars, beer mugs, clear tea cups, champagne flutes. Mr. S's desk had five glasses of water. I thought it odd that every now and then one of the glasses would just tip over and spill as if the world had tilted just for that one glass.

Back to the old house and now the glasses have been swapped with cheap clear plastic cups filled with water and a lot more of them. I got off the couch and wondered if the situation was the same at the new school, and sure enough, the same thing happened, maybe two or three clear plastic cups sat on each person's desk.

Suddenly, for a third time, I stood at my old home again, except the plastic cups contained an indigo liquid, Tru Blue. I panicked, filled with horror at my prior ignorance which allowed me to put myself in harm's way for such a long time. I ran to the door. When it opened, I stood in the new school's classroom; everyone sized me up just like when Mr. S. introduced me to the class, although now they had Tru Blue in plastic cups. About half of the cups tipped over, spilling blue liquid before I ran outside. Outside the door I stopped on a street corner, a massive city lay before me, the depth of which I knew stretched for miles, tall skyscraper behind tall skyscraper, an almost infinite amount of concrete. On the grey sidewalks and broken wood benches, plastic cups of Tru Blue spilled every few seconds. Tru Blue ran in the street's gutters. I ran and ran, turning one city street after another, the cups tipping over as soon as I saw them, but I couldn't stop running, I had to move or something bad would happen, and at the same time my movements and eyes caused the cups to spill. Avoiding the spills became impossible, eventually even the streets flowed with Tru Blue, all spilled from individual cups. I tripped on the slippery sidewalk and fell into the street, now a cerulean river swiftly flowing and too deep for me to touch the bottom. A thought, not my own, told me I need not struggle—if I relaxed all my muscles then I would float. And I didn't care whether or not the fact was true, I would kick and swim to the side, although I knew once I got there my options would be limited; cups continued to spill.

Kicking to stay afloat, I finally woke up in a sweat. I was unable to fall back asleep. I lay in bed, the sweat evaporating off my skin, thinking about the rapidly approaching day at the zoo and museum in the concrete city with my father.

CHAPTER ELEVEN

The warm airy hotel water hardly cleared the stale taste in my mouth nor did it refresh me for the challenges lying ahead. Jimmy seemed to have survived the night just fine, perhaps a little druggy. We ate breakfast at the hotel; my father added two creamers to his coffee. With a grey filled sky and a steady wind blowing, we drove to the caged animals in the city.

Zoos are strange places. Animals, some obviously quite intelligent, are caged and locked up, not just thousands of miles from their natural habitats, but in a completely different climate zone. Apparently, this zoo already decided to put away some of the animals for the winter. Who knows where they go, or how they feel about their indoor winter vacation starting in late fall. I remember a news story about a tiger at a zoo leaping out of her pit to attack a visitor who had taunted her minutes earlier. People discussed how zoos are wrong because of the incident. My father had made the comment that the tiger must have been female. When my Mom asked why, he responded that only a female could be so "vindictive" to only breakout for revenge when she had the opportunity to escape for so long. I had to look up "vindictive" on the internet.

Inside a giant humid building, we saw some snakes, pleased with tight confinement, and an alligator, rather unpleased with tight confinement. Only through reading the descriptions of the snakes could an onlooker learn which ones bit venom, unless a person had prior knowledge, of course. I thought that it would have been more appropriate for the zoo to have some sort of warning label or bright sticker on the outside of the glass tank for the dangerous snakes. Then again, I am sure the glass was thick.

Years prior I saw a venomous snake-handler. At first I could not believe the snake was indeed venomous, it must have been a sham, but my father assured me the claim was true, he knew the scaly pattern on the snake. How was this possible? My father said the handler had been handling the snake since it was born in order to acclimate the snake to human touch. And the handler always displayed confidence so as to never spook the serpent. I supposed this is how I would have to handle my father.

Not long after we entered the zoo, I realized that companies had sponsored each of the exhibits. The monkeys, where we spent a lot of time, had a famous banana brand next to their cage. I started to dread which animal would be next. What would Tru Blue sponsor: the dolphins, the sea otters, some exotic ants or bees? My father seemed to be on his phone, checking and sending messages, more than he watched the animals. I got bored too and remembered that on my new phone I could do more than text with Jamie and Ariel. I could update my Facebook, send emails, record a video, listen to music, etc... I decided to hang out with Dad and James a bit longer before I did that.

Surprisingly, the whole time we had planned on going to the zoo, I had not thought about the possibility of seeing them, but there they were, the most meaningful animal at the zoo, the elephants. My father never mentioned my windowsill roaming elephant, yet we lingered, watching the wrinkled enormous lumbering animals. Well, at least I appeared to be watching the elephants. Not long after we found a spot along the railing, lining the elephant pit, I noticed a bee buzzing around. A fairly innocuous and commonplace flying insect, a mere spec next to the exotic elephants. The bee mesmerized me. It fascinated me. Despite people's presumption of bees' constant industriousness, always collecting pollen for the hive, this bee buzzed along aimlessly. It didn't appear concerned about flowers, or even colorful clothing and hair that might be hiding pollen; it seemed lost, or, as I presumed, exploring. More importantly, I noticed that no one else watched the insect; everyone else either used their phones to text or talk, or focused on the elephants. So I followed it with my eyes, so as not to appear abnormal. I realized I would always have to monitor my own behavior, so as not to draw attention to myself and my new knowledge.

• • •

We had packed pizza for lunch; no doubt Tru Blue would be a part of that. We had lunch at a park downtown.

Leaves fell from the trees and the clouds had darkened, rain would surely fall soon. James guzzled down his soda; he was going to go for two again, pushing his luck since he seemed to feel the change in our father too.

"So there are a few museums downtown within walking distance from here. A fine art museum, that's the really old stuff, a modern art museum, and a children's museum."

"All of 'em."

"James we don't have time for all of them so we have to come to some agreement. I have to drop you guys off before six and the drive will take some time."

"Whatever you guys prefer."

"Maybe we could go to the children's museum today and another time check out the modern one, Eleanor."

"Ok, if that is what you think is best. Maybe James would like the modern art museum."

"I guess we could try to do both, they are right next to each other. You know what else is over there, the *Incantando* agency's office."

"Oh."

"Yeah it's the building next to the modern art. So how is that job going?"

"Oh, I haven't really done anything yet."

We threw away our trash. James started on another Tru Blue. I had a bottled-water which my father bought. At the zoo, I dumped it in the bathroom and refilled it.

"Dad, I really don't want to go to the kid's museum, maybe I could go by myself to the modern one?"

"Do you have your cell phone on you?"

"Of course, and it's charged."

"Alright, let's all walk to the modern one together and then James and I will keep walking to the children's one.

We'll meet you in your lobby at three-thirty."

"Ok."

"And keep track of time because your phone might not get service in the museum."

"Ok, Dad."

We walked in silence all the way to the modern museum. My feet ached and I was surprised that Jimmy didn't complain at all. My father bought me a ticket and repeated, again, everything he had said on the walk over. I took a stainless steel elevator up to the second floor; I needed to find a favorite painting for my plan to work. The museum had few patrons, so I jogged around a corner. The first thing I saw was a thin journal resting on a musical conductor's podium. A few pages from the beginning, the journal lay open. Set a few feet from the wall, a thin white tape lined the entire room. From behind this boundary I managed to read the words clearly:

Statement

I, Tehching, plan to do a One Year performance.

I will not do ART, not talk ART, not see ART, and not read ART for one year.

I will just live.

The performance will begin on February 24th 1995 and continue until February 24th 1996.

Signed,

_____

_____

Witness
New York City

The page was signed. He started his performance on my birthday, February 24th 1995. Despite the urgency, I continued to search the journal page. On the right side of the journal a writer had made impressions, barely visible, probably from another entry on the previous page. They were not deep enough to be legible. I took a glimpse around the room. Some photographs hung on the walls, no cameras hung on the ceiling. I took a step closer, crossing the tape on the ground. Nothing happened. I peered closer at the page. The signatures appeared real; the handwriting differed between the witnesses and the performer. And now I felt certain of another entry on the next page, but I still couldn't read it without flipping the page.

I started to move my right hand from my side, when a voice startled me, "please stay behind the line ma'am." An elderly white man with liver spots and a fragile frame covered by a navy blazer aggressively shuffled his feet and wiggled his shoulders at me.

"Oh, I'm sorry," I took a step back. I knew museum decorum, but I didn't want to play dumb. Instead I admitted my guilt, glancing down and blushing. I said, "I just wanted to see what he wrote on the previous page."

"You are not supposed to touch the exhibits in an art

museum young lady."

"I know."

"There's nothing there."

"What?"

"Nothing else is in the journal."

"But I can see words from the pen pushing down from the previous page."

"Have you seen the rest of the exhibit, you're at the end you know?"

"Yes"

"Then you know what else happens."

"Well yeah, but is that what he wrote in his journal."

He leaned forward and whispered, "I let you know a little secret." He glanced over his shoulder. "I looked."

"Oh."

"He didn't write anything else in this journal."

"Why would he leave the impressions on the page then?"

"Well, there could be any number of reasons, but I suspect they were notes about his purpose for the art work, or perhaps something more important."

"What do you think would be more important than his purpose?"

The old man hesitated for a moment and made a grimace as if he went to battle against pain older folks always seem to have. As soon as he spoke I knew my error, after his voice broke, he spoke with such vigor, that something else had to have caused the grimace.

"First of all, every piece of artwork has an author who produced it for some reason, but that is only the tip of understanding." The old man chewed his words as he spit them out, "and I suspect that if he did know any of the more powerful and important thoughts, he would rather thrash you with a stick than give away what took years for him to grasp!"

His face still calm, he clearly spoke for himself. I knew I had enough space to run away should I need to. Perhaps that's the reason I didn't feel threatened. Indifferent to my calm reaction, without further comment, he shuffled to the other end of the room, giving me plenty of space as he passed. I needed to get going. One piece would satisfy my father.

The elevator had not moved since I got out and I took the same one down and headed towards the exit. I took a right out the door, towards the children's museum, the entire sky steadily rained now. The ground smelt of wet asphalt, though it had not rained for some days. I didn't have an umbrella and my clothing wasn't warm enough for the drop in temperature. I jogged to the next building— grey, boring, tall.

Not being used to revolving doors, my heel caught the back of a door as someone was going out across from me going in. My ankle hurt, so I went to rub it.

"Watch it!" Someone almost ran me over coming in behind me. I straightened up abruptly, but the man sped away, already three steps ahead of me. I had no idea where to go, but I wanted to get out of the path of the revolving door since people seemed to have trouble seeing through it.

An older brown-haired man in a black suit with a black tie took a glance at me and then back at his computer. He sat on a small chair which probably made him taller sitting than standing. Knowing his voice would carry he spoke in a normal voice, "may I help you?"

"Yes, umm, I am trying to find this ad company."

"Ok, do you know the name of the company?"

"Um, yeah, ah, it's *Incantado*, Italian for 'enchanting'." The man glimpsed down at his screen again. "I've checked under "I" and "E" and don't see anything similar."

"It's with an "*I*.""

"Emm, nope, sorry, are you sure you are at the right address."

"No, Ok, I will try next door."

A man and woman were leaving the building in a hurry so I thought I would try to get behind them out the door. I almost bumped into the man as he gestured for the lady to go first between the doors. I kept close to him and at the last instant decided not to hop into the doors with him. The next door went around and I followed it as closely as I could.

The rain poured so much I didn't even feel the cold. I tried the street on the other side of the art museum. By the time I crossed to the next grey, boring, and tall building, my clothes felt heavy, soaked in water.

This time I had no problem with the revolving doors. A very well-dressed business man, almost intimidating in such a well cut, form-fitting suit, came out of a glass door near the revolving ones and I slipped in behind him. In front of me, but facing the center of the lobby, glared two screens inside a large concrete table. A man was dancing his fingers on the concrete just below the screens. As I approached the concrete table keyboards became visible. On a robin's-egg-blue screen, below the word "DIRECTORY," a long white rectangle had a blinking dash. I typed "I." Pushing the down arrow I found *Incantando* suite 700.

When I turned around I noticed for the first time that the lobby was completely made of concrete. On the middle of the wall facing the revolving doors hung a dark painting. As I walked towards where the elevators must be, I couldn't stop staring at the painting.

Against a dark, nearly black background, a man, his mouth open screaming in agony, sat on a melting chair surrounded by a purple veil. Why would someone put that in a lobby? His expression typified agony, but his hands were calm and complacent, casually resting on the arm chair. Nothing seemed to be causing the pain; he was melting, but so were the veil and the chair. The streaks of purple really caught my eye.

I pressed the up button and waited for one of the dozen elevators. The tone that announced the arrival of an elevator sounded off, a little deeper and less chirpy. No one came out of the elevator and no one came in with me. At the seventh floor I walked out and looked right, a wall. I checked left, another wall. After going straight, I took the first right I could and discovered the familiar door, which I opened confidently. A mother and child sat in the waiting room. I suspect they appeared much like my mom and I, although the child was clearly younger. Neither of them took any notice of me. Again, no one sat at the tiny front desk, its computer screen off.

Slowly, I walked straight back to the rest of the office. As I exited the waiting room the hallway stretched out to my right. I took a breath and turned the corner with poise. No one occupied the hallway, which seemed to signal that someone would soon be approaching.

On the right were the two doors to the bathroom. The room I had seen before lay further down and on the left.

The door was closed. When I got there I stood and listened. No sound came from the room or any other room, so I checked the door. It was unlocked.

I pushed it inwards and stepped inside. A long black shiny table with about a dozen chairs filled the room. Black matching cabinets lined the back wall. Peeking in the cabinets, I saw nothing unusual, just some paper, staplers, tape, empty folders, and other office supplies. As I flipped through the folders, I kept glancing back at the door. Although I was still a little wet from outside, I started to sweat.

Not until I stood back in the hallway, did I decide to go deeper. The hallway took a left. As I turned the corner someone flashed across in front of me at the other end of the hall. About five doors separated us, and he turned down another hallway, away from Michelle's office.

I wanted to listen to each door and check the handles before attempting to enter. At the first door on my right I didn't hear anything. Patiently, I slowly wrapped my fingers around the cold handle before I pressed down. After giving way for a bit, the handle stopped, the door was locked. At the very next door, still on my right, I could hear something. Someone was speaking. Then there was music. All the while I could hear that slight hum of a television. The carpet underneath the door flickered light. As I went to grab the door handle, simply to check the lock, the door behind me swung open and a man wearing black slacks and a white dress shirt shot out walking the opposite way down the hall. Again they paid no notice to me; he even left the door hanging open in the hallway. I slowly went to the now open door and listened. Without touching the door I made my way around it. No one occupied the small dark room. A soft light poured in from one of the walls. I stepped in, it smelled sterile.

The light came from the next room where a small child sat on a fluffy tan loveseat watching television. He had to be about Jimmy's age, five or six. The room where I stood had two office-like swivel chairs and a small table with two computer monitors displaying numerous graphs, lines moving left to right like a heartbeat. One of the screens had a small close-up video-feed of the child's face. I glimpsed back at the child on the couch. The child, couch, and TV were sideways to me and the child did not notice that I had entered the room next to him. This had to be one-way glass. I could not see a camera on top of the TV, only a black box the same color as the TV.

That's when I noticed that the child wore a headband with wires coming out of it. The computer screens had moving graphs. I had to get out of there. I knew of an excuse I could use in the hallway, but what could I say if I was discovered in here? Then the door opened and a man walked in behind the child in the loveseat.

"Hey Kevin," the voice was clear, but came from a speaker on the desk, not from where the man was standing in the room, "I think one of the sensors is falling off there buddy."

The child just sat facing the TV screen and never looked back at the man.

"Okaaay." His little voice sounded clear too, coming from the speakers on the desk.

The man approached the boy with his hands outstretched. He started fiddling with the headband. "Ok, that should do it."

He started back towards the door. I quickly sought a

place to hide. There was nothing. He would surely see me under the desk. I glanced into the TV room again. Just as his last foot was leaving the room, it paused, and the man came back in with a funny look on his face. He headed straight for me behind the mirror. I froze, although I'm sure he couldn't see me. He then leaned down out of sight of the window. I ran out of the room and around the corner. I stopped in front of the women's bathroom. I waited in the hall, my heart pounding.

After a minute, I decided to peer around the corner, but that would appear suspicious. So, I casually walked around the corner trying to look natural. Both doors were shut; he must have been behind the one-way mirror again.

I went deeper. I listened to the next closed door on the left side of the hall and checked—unlocked. I really wanted to get out of that hall so I slowly and smoothly opened the door. The room was all white. I opened the door further. As I stepped into the room, the door no longer blocked my view, and I saw a woman in a white lab coat sitting behind a panel of screens, dials, and switches with her back to me. She didn't seem to notice that I had entered the room. Around her blond hair some old-school headphones covered her ears. Behind me the door closed almost silently, except a slight click which made me cringe.

"How are you doing?"

I froze in place. My mouth was open; my hands dangled by my sides.

"Ok, well just a few more, Ok?"

Without moving my feet I leaned to my left to look around the woman. I didn't see anything merely a big white wall. I took a step to my left. The back wall was actually a massive machine. A hole, nearly the size of an opening to a large dog house, illuminated by soft ultra-white lights, had a pair of grey kid-sized sneakers, designed for skating, sticking up and out from a foot.

The door behind me clicked open and a man entered. A twisted expression of surprise came over the man's face. His large mouth dropped open showing crooked bottom teeth and his brown eyes widened. He wore red rimmed glasses and a white lab coat. He quickly shut his mouth, narrowed his eyes on me and backed-up as he motioned me with his finger. He stepped out of the room, but kept the door open with his right hand for me to follow.

"A little too excited are we?"

I stood silent.

"You must be Kat."

The door clicked shut behind me and I jumped.

"Please stay in the waiting room dear, you will get to go in, just be patient."

He smiled with his perfect white upper teeth. I started to walk back to the waiting room and decided to turn and add an, "ok." He went back into the room. Once I went around the first corner I picked up my pace to a fast walk. I passed the conference room that was once awash in indigo light and vibrations. When I got to the waiting room, one of the women looked up from her magazine. I froze again. She stared back at the magazine in her lap.

In the elevator I felt grateful to be alone again. I don't even remember walking back to the modern art museum or how much it rained, if any. I glanced at my cell phone and realized I still had thirty minutes. My ticket was still valid so I wandered around the museum shop. Nothing kept my interest as I tried to compute what I had just seen.

My father arrived early in the lobby. Jimmy sat on a

bench and my father stood. Again he didn't really look at me. "So you have a good time?"

"Yes," and with that we started out the door.

"What was your favorite piece?"

I described the journal. "What's the name of the artist?" Phonetically I said, "Teching, like "teaching" but without the "*a.*" That's his first name though; I can't remember his last name."

"Well that's the one you need to know sweetie."

"I know."

"Elly, Jimmy is getting a bit tired; I think it's time to go back to Mother's alright?"

"Ok," I couldn't believe he just referred to our house that way.

We hastily walked to the car in sprinkling rain. No one said a word nearly the whole way there until my father broke the silence, "how could anyone not see art for a whole year?"

I thought about the exhibit and ventured a guess, "well there was a photograph of a prison cell."

"Oh, ok, so he locked himself up for a year. I mean cause, you couldn't look anywhere." My brother and I had our heads down and shoulders hunched trying not to get sprinkled on. I took a glance at my father; his head was up and attentive, his eyes blinking to fight off the small drops. So I did the same, and I finally saw that we were not on a grey rainy city street; we walked surrounded in a dense jungle of *colors*: growing out of first floor shops, hanging out windows, on top of cabs, splattered on people.

"I suppose it depends on your definition of what *art* means. Did he explain that in the journal?"

"Nope, I told you everything that he wrote," and the

thought surfaced—are advertisements art?

"Well, I guess he wouldn't have to explain what he meant by art for that year since he said he wouldn't speak about art either."

"That's even if he did it."

"Good point Eleanor, most people never follow through on things they say anyways," a touch of bitterness carried through the rain.

"Well, I'd believe him if he was in prison."

"I don't even know about that, they have cable TV in prison nowadays, Elly."

"Well you don't have to watch it if you don't want to, right?"

"I don't know."

As we were getting into the car, I figured I better ask about their time at the children's museum. My dad said he liked it, even though I am positive he was on his phone most of the time. Surprisingly, James didn't say much.

"I liked it more than the zoo. It was cool that I got to play with things."

Before we even left the parking garage Jimmy had fallen asleep. My father drove in silence. I don't think the Agency had contacted him about me at their office. Once we exited the highway, he started again. "Eleanor, I don't know if things will be going back to normal anytime soon."

We stopped in a turning lane waiting for a light. "What's going on has nothing to do with you and little Jimmy. Your mom and I really need to spend some time apart now."

He reached under his seat, got a water bottle, cracked it open and took a sip.

"If you ever want to talk with me or your mom, just say so. You can call me any time. Did you have a good time today?"

"Yes."

"Good, good. I can't remember the last time we got to talk like we did last night at dinner. It was fun today too, huh?"

I gave a weak, "yeah."

When we got to the house he pulled in the drive way and all of us got out. My father grabbed both of our bags and he knocked on the door. He turned back at us and looked up at the sky as he spoke, "alright, well, your mom's not home. You kids going to be alright?"

"Sure."

He handed us our bags. For a second all of us simply stood there. Then I started to feel through my front pocket for my keys to the house. I let James and me into the house. We said our goodbyes. His hug still seemed unusual and foreign. He didn't attempt to force me to drink Tru Blue though.

James went to his room and I tried to find out more on the internet. I tried researching more about viruses. The more I read, or rather the more I tried to read, the more that I realized this stuff was incredibly complicated. How could I possibly understand it when I couldn't understand half the words in each sentence? I couldn't specifically read about viruses. I had to read about how the human body worked. And not merely the body, but organs, individual cells, systems, and I couldn't comprehend even half the vocabulary. Mostly, my eyes just stared at the page.

My mother didn't explain where she came from when she arrived around thirty minutes later. She asked about our day during dinner. I didn't tell her what I saw at the Agency.

After desert my mom surprised me, "I did some research earlier today online."

"Oh, yeah."

"I think we're going to have a great day shopping tomorrow with Macy."

I had forgotten all about the shop-along. Desperately, I wanted to cancel, but when I looked at my mother's crow's feet around her eyes and the hard creases coming down from the corners of her rouged lipstick lips, I knew it would be a tough battle. Any tactic I took, from feigning an illness to being honest about what I thought about the Agency, Macy and Michelle, would be met with more and more questions and arguments. She would know I lied about being ill and she would get to the bottom of my issues with the Agency. Eventually, I could get her to cancel the shopping trip, but the cost would be her judgement of me: Eleanor is not adjusting to her new situation at school and her parents' impending divorce. Which would mean she would treat me as a child, a weak-minded, overly sensitive child, for months or years. So I said nothing.

I had gone for a walk once during twilight and a few other times in the dark after dinner. I found that it cleared my mind and I enjoyed looking at the stars although the light pollution was bad. The regular intervals of the streetlights, along with the cookie-cutter houses formed a kind of geometric pattern, complicated enough to not easily solve, and so mundane I had no interest in determining the pattern. I walked in the center of the street. There were no cars, no sound of cars, and clouds must have blanketed the sky because there were no stars. The shadowy outlines of trees, the quiet doorways, and the beige lights created a sort of walking-hypnosis. I was cold; I hadn't dressed warm enough. No amount of walking seemed to warm me. Gradually, the houses got darker and darker—no light above the doors, no light coming from the windows. The black spaces increased between the streetlights, leaving large patches of obscurity. The power must have gone out. I turned around to head back and saw nothing, just black, empty darkness. I turned around again—no lights. I felt cold and could see my breath. My mom's voice called me from the distance, "Eleanor!"

I called back, but I could tell from her voice that she had not heard me. I double backed into the darkness. From the echoing sounds of my steps, I felt the shallow canyon of nondescript houses and their splintered wood fences. My mom called out again, closer, "Eleanor where are you?"

I could hear the strain in her voice, which agitated me, and I answered impatiently, "coming Mom!"

Somehow she still seemed not to hear me, although she was closer, and no longer yelling, "where are you dear?"

I stopped in the middle of the street. The tight strain in her voice wasn't stress or worry, but a hollow pitch, as if someone was forcing her. I spoke quietly to myself into the darkness, "Mom?"

"Eleanor, my dear, you are so close, why don't you join us?" Her voice sneered cynical, a mock caring, and had a sharp tightness like she was carrying something really heavy.

"Mother, is it you?"

"Of course, dear," her voice came from the darkness

directly in front of me, but too high off the ground, "come here I want to buy you something."

In front of me came the sound of water rushing down a drain. A tattered figure in white, loose feet dangling off the ground, my mother floated towards me with her chest pushed out and her head cocked to the side unnaturally, as if she were dead.

I woke with my clammy damp forehead pressed hard against the pillow lying in my bed. I was shivering with the covers kicked off. At first I still felt disoriented, like I was waking from one dream into another because the room seemed so alien to me. As my breathing returned to normal, I heard an electrical humming stop, and I thought the dream had been transmitted to me, but as I woke up more, my head cleared and I realized the idea had been just as irrational as the dream.

CHAPTER TWELVE

Experiencing consciousness the next morning felt fine and normal for about three to five seconds. Then my situation came to me in a flash. I jumped out of bed and went to the kitchen for a packet of oatmeal and some mushy apricots. My mother was fixing breakfast for Jimmy, when she glanced over at me, "are you excited about today Eleanor?"

"Yeah sure."

Jimmy and Mom were both eating cereal from a box with a cartoon on it that Jimmy sometimes watched on TV. A milk jug and an orange juice container, both with screw-on caps stood in the middle of the table between us. Mom had a coffee and Jimmy a glass of orange juice. I had been checking the garbage compactor for small creamers, but never found any. My mom seemed to be using a half-and-half carton in the fridge.

"See, I toooold you this would be the best tasting cereal ever."

My Mother cackled a "ha" and glanced over at me.

"The cereal has shapes of Jimmy's favorite cartoon," she finished looking down at Jimmy, "but it's the same recipe honey."

"No, it's better Mom," and in his cartoon voice he added, "parents just don't know."

"They said that it's enriched with vitamins…" She picked up the box and read the side.

Jimmy seemed antagonistic, "they're just for kids, Mom."

"Enriched?"

"Yeah, that's what the commercials say."

"Does the same company make Tru Blue soda?"

"No, no I wouldn't think so," my mother looked up at me. "Why?"

"Oh, nothing."

"Is it you?"

I stared at my mother. She acted as if she didn't even ask me a question. Finally, she commented, "you know sweetie, you can wear some makeup today if you'd like."

I immediately thought of the rings under my eyes, "ok."

"It's always a good idea to dress nice when shopping for nice clothes."

Mother followed Jimmy into his room. When she came out a few minutes later she reminded me that we had thirty minutes. When I went into the bathroom I really noticed my eyes. I guess I hadn't been sleeping well the last few nights.

I picked out some of my better clothes. The day seemed clear and the air cold when I checked out the front-door, but my mom told me it should be unseasonably warm. I decided to go with my designer jeans and a light denim jacket, also a big fashion name, with a long-sleeve solid-red shirt underneath.

I let James have the front seat. On the way to Jimmy's friend's birthday party we had to pick up a gift. Just as we pulled into a parking lot James started asking, "Mommy, let's get Shane the new Tru Blue?"

"The new soda?"

"Yeah."

"Honey, that's not a good present."

"Maybe he hasn't tried it yet."

"You two really like that stuff, huh?" she glanced back at me in the rearview mirror but quickly went back to watching the road. "Jimmy, you can't get someone soda for a birthday present."

"Why not?"

"Well, it won't last sweetie. You want a present that will last."

"What do you mean?"

"All you boys will probably drink all the soda today and then Shane won't even have any. We're already at the store. Elly, you want to come in too."

I elected to stay in the car in the backseat. I could feel the texture of the seat beneath my hands as a sigh of relief escaped my mouth. I watched as people went in and out. Some carried plastic soda bottles of Tru Blue, with the slogan facing me: Is it you? One kid even had a long sleeve shirt with the logo of the soda.

It was staged. They planned on having the Tru Blue present conversation; they waited for the parking lot so that I would be sure to hear it over the sound of the car and the road. I thought to myself that they must have great plans for me.

Suddenly they were back with a wrapped present and

we were off. The neighborhood of James's friend seemed like ours, yet something felt different. Maybe the houses had been painted darker? Or the grass grew a lighter color, perhaps a different variety? The trees stood the same size. Having a sense of direction is difficult in this new suburb. Who knows, maybe this was my neighborhood?

"I'm going to go in with James to meet Shane's parents, ok sweetie?"

"I'll stay here Mom."

They left me in the car, crossed the street, and went into the next house in front of me. Minutes after they were gone, I felt someone staring at me. I turned to my right and a boy James' age, with brown hair, brown eyes, and a funny stubby nose, stood gawking at me. He widened his eyes, lifted his upper lip revealing his teeth, chortled and then jiggled his head before he ran in front of the car and off towards the house. He carried a present with a pattern and color scheme much like the one James had. The wrapper had logos of Tru Blue on the clothes of young boys jumping bikes and skateboards every which way in some swirling white and cerulean landscape. Weren't boys jumping bikes and skateboards on James present too?

Suddenly the driver's door opened, "honey, don't you want to ride up front?" I moved to the front. "Well, it's great that James got invited to this party. Hopefully he meets some more friends there."

We rode in silence to the freeway.

"Don't you want to know where we are going shopping today?"

"Oh, no not really." I thought for a moment, "I trust you Mom."

"Thanks sweetie," my mother smiled. "That reminds

me, we will be meeting with Macy from your work in about an hour."

"Oh."

"We'll probably have some time to go to one store together. I don't know too much about what Macy has planned, do you?"

"No, none at all."

"Well, apparently she'll be giving you some spending cash, pretty cool huh?"

"Yeah, I guess so."

"What's bothering you hon? Did you just want to have it be the two of us, like we usually do?"

"No, nothing's wrong, Mom."

"Is it the problem between your dad and me?"

"Ah, yeah, that's been bothering me a bit."

"Would you like to talk about it?"

"Hmm, I don't really know what to say."

"Elly, you know your father and I both love you."

After a beat my mother questioned, "Elly?"

"Yes, of course I know that Mom."

She then continued saying the same exact things she said before: the situation had nothing to do with James and me; this is not really so sudden; things had been going bad for them for a time, etc… I didn't really add anything, it was more of a speech. As we exited the highway she finally dropped the subject and quit talking to herself.

"Ok, left here right?"

"Correct."

"Then what?"

"Then go straight for point seven miles and take a left onto Harding."

"Ok, so how is school going?"

"Alright."

"Yeah, so are you making friends?"

"Yeah, sort of."

"Hmm, I would have expected you to have had some friends over by now."

"Oh well."

"Not that there is anything wrong with that, Elly. I know we moved and this is your first time moving and everything, but maybe you could…" Somewhat annoyed I stopped her, "Mom."

Sensing my annoyance my mom responded, "what sweetie?"

"So I have this group project in history, one of the boys is really cute."

"Oh yeah?"

"So I want to try really hard to do a good job on the presentation."

"Oh, that's a good idea."

"We have to have some props and so we're like performing a few skits. We have one planned where I'll play a witch that's being burned at the stake."

"What kind of presentation is this on?"

"Our topic is colonial American punishments."

"Oh, that sounds interesting. Which way now?"

"Take a left onto Harding. So I was trying to come up with something to say to the class during the skit. You know, like pretending they are the mob set to burn me and I put a curse on them."

"Oh honey, you don't want to do that."

"What?"

"Put a curse on your classmates, you just moved here. You want to stay positive."

"But Mom it's not like a real curse or anything."

"Elly, they may not get the joke."

"But it's not a joke; it's a part of the skit."

"Elly, I don't think you should be negative, you want to make a good impression with your classmates."

"Mom, it's not like the first day for me or anything. I know most of the people in that class by name and I think most of them know me," although I wasn't so sure concerning the last part.

"Maybe you should just think of something else. I mean do you, like, have to be burned alive? Couldn't you simply perform a skit of the trial?"

"The trial?"

"Yeah, the trial," she flicked her eyes at me, "I think you better do some more research."

My face started to get a little heated, "I guess since I spoke with Dad about the tar and feathering that I sort of pictured an angry mob for witches too."

"Maybe they did mobs, but there were famous witch trials, held in courts." I did not make a sound and Mom gave me her car-driving-glance where she grips the steering wheel and glares at me to see my reaction. She seemed angry, "court, Eleanor, that's where highly intelligent men deliberate, and there's rules, and witnesses," I didn't make a sound again but she didn't glare at me, her tone got more frustrated, "and there is cross-examination and, its justice, the highest justice human beings can come up with, and that's the opposite of mob justice."

"Ok."

We rode silently until the car turned and my mom had cooled down, "help me find parking."

My mother and I went into only one shop before she

decided we had better eat before meeting Macy. We found a sandwich place; our last city had a few of these franchises too, which had some outdoor seating. Mom reasoned that it would be an opportunity before winter to eat outside and it had warmed up considerably. Both of us ordered water; my mom waited for me to choose what to drink before she made her choice.

At lunch Mom sat calm and contemplative which was fine with me because I was too. I doubt we thought about the same things though. After I finished my sandwich I confronted Mom with the question that revealed a lot about Dad.

"When I told Dad about, like, the history presentation, we started talking about why witches were burned alive, and Dad said that it was done to women who were independent and, like, smart." My mom had set her sandwich down and stared intently at me. I couldn't finish my sentence while looking at her so I spoke to my sandwich wrapper—*The Last Best and Honest Sandwich Place*—"...and then he like said something about that being the reason for the high amounts of divorces in the U.S."

A wind started to rustle through our printed wax paper. "Oh honey, no, your father and I, well, your father never wanted me to be, nor am I, a dependent person."

My mouth was dry and had a lingering taste of mustard. "No, he didn't say that was, ah, the problem or anything."

"Sometimes people just grow apart."

"That's not really what I mean." I had to drop my eyes at the wrapper again, "I mean..."

She spoke right at me, "Elly, we're going to be fine," and took a sip of her cup of water.

"Ok, Mom."

"Now we should probably get going, I told Macy we'd meet her in ten minutes."

When we finished, we set out to meet Macy outside a shop. I could see her from afar, about four stores down. She searched in our direction, but instead of showing signs of recognition, she stared straight down at her cell phone and started clicking away. Unlike when we first met, Macy was dressed casually chic. She had on flats in three tones of brown, designer denim jeans, and a cute long-sleeve blue-green tight V-neck light sweater which matched her expensive designer handbag and hazel eyes well.

My mom barely seemed to notice that I was slowing down, "hello Macy."

"Oh this is Macy."

"Hello there. You must be Emily. It's a pleasure to meet you."

"And it's a pleasure to meet you too."

"How are you doing Eleanor?"

Trying to sound cheerful, I said, "alright"

"Macy, I must say I didn't think this is what you hired Elly for."

"Oh, well, she has been doing some other stuff for us as well." Her voice seemed a bit shaky and she fidgeted in place. "Um, so I guess I should explain a little bit," Macy paused. She smiled, perhaps a little nervously, as she went on. "Well, we'd like to follow you around for a bit as you shop. I'll be making a few notes on a pad of paper and I might ask you a few questions. The best part," she gave a short pause, "we're giving you one-hundred dollars."

Forcing a smile I got out a "cool."

"So I do have a few questions before we get started."

She gave my mom a nervous look and my mother quickly agreed.

Macy turned her gaze on me. "How did you pick where we would be shopping today?"

"Oh, well, Mom did." Macy got out a small pad of paper and a pen from her purse. "Tell her what you told me in the car, Elly."

"Um," I wasn't sure what she meant. "Oh, I trust that my mom would pick out a good place to shop."

"How often do you two shop together and apart?"

"Oh, I would say Elly and I are together more than half the time, although I would say, Elly buys most of her clothes with me, wouldn't you Elly?" Although the question had been directed to me, my mom's answer only seemed to endear Macy instead of annoying her.

"Yeah, when I just go with my friends I usually only buy, like, accessories."

"Could you give me, say, a percentage of time you two shop together?"

"Well, in the last year or so, where we used to live and I have a lot of girlfriends, I maybe shopped sixty percent of the time with my mom, especially for clothes."

"Um-k, just one last question. Have you girls had lunch yet?"

"Yes we recently finished. Are you hungry?"

"No I'm good; I just had a bit of a snack. Where did you two go and what did you order?"

My mom forgot her cup of water and I deliberately forgot to mention what I had to drink. Throughout the day, Macy had very placid facial expressions; she never smiled nor frowned at anything my mom or I said. She didn't miss the drinks, "and what did you have to drink?"

"Oh, only water."

"What kind did they have?"

"We had some from the tap."

"Ok, that should do it. Now it's totally up to you Eleanor, whatever you'd do today as if I wasn't here."

"Eleanor saw some of the shops in the car and I am not sure that I would like to go to them. And I am sure there are some shops you wouldn't like to visit with me."

"Ok, let's split up Mom."

"Let's say we met back here in one hour." My mom checked her purse. "It was nice meeting you Macy. I guess I will see you two in one hour then."

"Nice meeting you too."

My mom turned her back on me and went the direction we had come from. Although she is only three inches taller than me, Macy had a slight yet noticeably growing smile. This would be the last smile for some time. I showed her the paper my mom had printed out for me.

"Ok, where would you like to go to first?"

"Um, let's go to the nearest one."

We started walking. Macy avoided a group of people by walking me even closer to the wall. She continued with her questioning, "do you and your mom often split up when you shop together?"

"Um, yeah, usually if we spend the afternoon shopping we will split for an hour or so."

"And where do you usually get the money to spend."

"Oh, well, I help out around the house. I sort of babysit my brother and other things. Sometimes Mother will take me shopping for getting good grades, but she likes to *insist* that it's not for good grades, but, like, finishing the year or semester or something."

Macy's face was non-expressive again. Every now and then I would check her reactions to my words. She never once seemed pleased, discouraged, excited, or amused. Usually people at least smile when I tell them how my mom always takes me out for good grades, but pretends we are going out for something else. Macy did seem positive. And she did seem to like me.

She opened the heavy glass door for me with surprising ease. Once inside I headed to my right. It appeared to be a part of the women's section in a jeans store. Macy didn't follow me; she went to the left as we entered. I wasn't sure what to do. I kept thinking to myself—act natural.

As I moved from rack to rack, I glanced at Macy. She pretended to inspect various pairs of pants, holding them up towards me and fingering their labels; however, every now and then she would take glances at me. When I moved farther into the shop she followed my trail of racks and clothes. Sometimes she held her phone towards me and pretended to text. I finally found some jeans in the color I wanted. I just need to find the right amount of fade. An assistant came over and asked if everything was ok.

"Well, there's nothing you could help me with."

I wasn't sure if Macy wanted me to say anything or not, but I found something, and I thought I might ask her. She seemed absorbed in a jean jacket, not particularly happy or sad, but occupied. So, I went into the changing room. The lights were harsh. In the full mirror I took a long look at myself before I did anything else. My eyes still looked tired even with makeup. I started thinking of Anita. She had permanent black circles around her eyes, her whole family did. They were a second generation from some Eastern

European country. At least my eyes were not that bad.

I don't really remember how the jeans fit. When I finished, I folded the jeans the way they were before and put them back on a different shelf. Halfway to walking to Macy, she glanced up at me expressionless and then looked back down, not recognizing my motion to her. So, I kept walking out of the store.

Once out of sight of the shop's windows I waited for her. "Thanks for waiting; by the way, some stores are not with us." Not sure of what to say, I stood silent. "I should have told you that before we went in. Try not to be so worried about me, just shop like you normally would. So, what's next?"

I named another store.

"Ok, it's best if I don't interact with you in that shop either." We started walking. "But when we meet up with your mom, it should be fine. That department store is alright with us. I would film you there, but I forgot my video-camera in the car." I walked silently next to her. What should have I said to that?

"So I noticed you spent a lot of time checking out the shirts that give some of the proceeds to AIDS patients in Africa." I hadn't really noticed anything, except for Macy watching me. "Um, yeah."

"When you approached the rack at what point did you realize some of the proceeds would go to Africa?"

"Um, as I walked towards it."

"Did you read the sign or did you remember the red-label brand and recognize it that way?"

"Um, in the store."

"And it wasn't the pattern of the shirts that first interested you in that particular rack?"

"Ah, no."

"You know that this is, like, just some observation, Eleanor. You're not going to lose your job or anything like that."

"Yes."

"Ok, so you don't need to be nervous or anything."

"Ok."

"So feel free to simply talk with me. I am not judging."

"Ok."

"I also noticed you put back the jeans you tried on."

"Um yeah."

"How come you did that?"

"Oh, so if I don't find anything later, we can go back to that store and we'll be able to find that pair again."

Before we reached the next planned shop, I noticed a store display with some shoes. As I slowed down to look at them, Macy came to a stop and then I did too. When I checked with Macy to see if it was acceptable to her if we made this little detour, she wasn't looking at the shoes but staring at my face already.

"Um, is it…"

She anticipated my question, "of course, wherever you'd like to go, this is your show."

I headed for the door. "Do you usually shop with a list of shops?"

"Oh no, it's only because we recently moved here and everything. The list would save Mom and I time."

I found the section inside the store that had the shoes on display. "So normally you go to a mall or a shopping area and walk around then?"

"Oh well, yeah, we knew the places to go and would just go. I don't know how or when exactly I learned, but I bet I could drive to most of them and I still have a year until I get a car."

I checked the price on the shoe that caught my eye and a few more around it. Not heeding Macy's advice, since she stood directly over me, I checked if she had finished. She already focused on me again and gave me a slight curled lip smile. She didn't leave at the same time as me; I had to wait for her again around the corner of the store.

Not hearing the shuffling of feet, smelling the sour breath, or seeing the dirty brown jacket, a voice of a homeless man suddenly came from beside me, not further than a person's length away from my body.

"I... I..." he took a step closer and I got a whiff of his sour breath, "want, ah argh, would you..." He spoke at a normal tempo. I gestured at him that I had no money to spare. "Just listen, I want, would like to tell..." Then his face gave off such an intensity of expression, his dirty mouth grimaced, his eyes brightened. "They *examined* me, said I wasn't," he got a little slurry, "able to function in society."

I felt positive that I could move faster than him if he went to grab me. He continued, pronouncing to anyone listening. "This coming from someone who cuts up *dead bodies*." His voice shook, I started to inch away still facing him. "Yeah, I know *their* past; they used to pay for dug-up freshly buried corpses, yes, yes uh-huh, under threat of burning death."

"Hey, get out of here!" Macy approached us at a trot.

"I don't want, argh, wouldn't like, any of your *change*."

Macy's trot slowed to a fast walk, took me by the arm, and we kept going. I gave a peek over my shoulder at the homeless man. He spoke a little louder. "I would like a job!

I want in!" He lowered his voice with each sentence and our distance doubled the effect. "Sign me up. Let me join. I would like to drink from the cup."

For the first time that afternoon, Macy finally gave some expression to her voice, "what a poor guy!" We took a few more steps, putting distance from the homeless man. She started on me again, expressionless, "so was forty dollars too much for those shoes?"

"No, um, I liked them. Ah, they were kinda sporty, outdoorsy and cute."

"Why didn't you want to buy them?"

As so often, the memory of the homeless man faded quickly. "Oh, I already have some sporty white sneakers and a darker brown skate shoe that I would probably wear instead of those. I also already have some flats, but they're not brown and outdoorsy. And so it just wasn't different enough from some of the other stuff I have at home."

"Very good. You'll have to show me your shoe collection when we get to your house."

"What!?" I began to lose composure.

"Oh my God, I don't think I asked you or your mom yet." For the second time, she showed some emotion. She seemed genuinely displeased with herself. "Ok, um, yeah, so like would it be ok if I come over after we are done shopping, if it's not too late?"

"Ah."

"You know, so I could see what you already have to get a better idea about today?"

"Ah, ok."

Macy stopped, "oops, we passed it up." She turned and then stopped again. "You go ahead, I'll be right behind you."

And she was. This shop marketed towards preteens and teens like me; our old city had one too. I would normally spend a much longer time in the store, but we would have to meet with Mom and I had this feeling and hope that she could do something about Macy. The experience in the store went the same as the others. Macy kept her distance and faced me while she texted or inspected some item. The only different behavior from Macy occurred when she took out her notepad for a minute and bought a bracelet from a basket that I spent some time going through. She even got the red one that I almost bought. I did buy some stuff this time, some jeans, a cute newspaper-girl hat in a dark, tightly patterned plaid, and a little joke book for my brother. I did have one-hundred bucks to spend after all.

Macy stood in line behind the person behind me, so I waited around the corner again. She asked the same questions and some new ones. "What did you think of the guy behind the cash register?"

"He was kinda old?"

Macy let out a little laugh. I felt a little more comfortable even though I don't know why she laughed. I went on, "his hair was too long, I think, and a little greasy. With that shaggy cut he really needs to keep it out of his eyes more. He was, like, rude too; he kinda snatched my stuff out of my hand."

Macy kept a smile on her lips as we walked a little further, heading to the department store. "Yeah, I think he broke their age policy. He must be a manager if he is over twenty-two."

"What do you mean?"

"Oh, just that he must have been working there for a while to be so old. Or they must be understaffed."

I started thinking of ways to get some information from Macy. I couldn't just ask her about Tru Blue directly, only if I could come up with a way to get her to start talking about it. At the entrance, my mom waited with a smile and two bags in her hands.

"How are you?"

"Good, how are you two doing?"

"Good," Macy turned to me, "it's going well."

"Ok, well I think this will be the last store for the day, huh? We need to pick up Jimmy in two hours."

"Oh, Emily, I am so sorry that I forgot to mention it earlier and I only remember because it came up with Eleanor, but would it be ok if I came over and got a tour of Eleanor's room?"

"Um, well I don't see why not." I felt deflated. I wasn't looking at my mom as she conversed with Macy, but if I had, she would have saw my lips tremble in despair.

"You see, it's kind of part of the shop-along process," Macy practically rambled, "because I would look into Eleanor's closet and have her explain to me why she bought what she bought today and how it relates to what she already has."

"Oh, I see, that makes perfect sense. Yes, of course, that would make sense, but, ah, Elly how do feel about that?"

I frowned at my mom, "um, it's ok, I guess."

"Great, so you'll follow us?"

"I have GPS in the car so I could just enter your address."

One last store, we stopped barely inside the doors and decompressed.

"Now we only have so much time before we have to

pick up Jimmy. Do you want to go towards the makeup and shoes, Elly?"

"Sure."

We passed the men's section and then the lingerie with Macy right behind my mom and me. Once we got to the women's shoes, I stuck close to my mom. My mom asked my opinion on a few shoes; I noticed a theme of black in her selections. She always seemed to find at least one thing wrong with each pair; the heel seemed too big; exactly like the one at home; the tips too flat; the tips too pointy. If I said that I liked a pair, she would spend more time studying it. Once my mom glanced back at Macy and Macy just said to pretend that she wasn't there. My mom had an easier time with that than me. My mom never gave her opinion when I picked out a pair for myself.

While we waited for a pair to be brought out for her, I stared off into space. Macy asked in a soft voice, "what do you think of that ad?" Apparently I was staring at a poster ad. I hadn't really noticed it.

A pair of glossy light red lips barely parted and curled into a sensual smile on a small poster on a stand near the makeup counter. The name of the brand shone in metallic cursive at the right bottom corner. My mom had turned to look, "I like it. They're attractive." She stayed twisted in her chair.

Macy's head turned back to me. I said the first thing that came to my mind, "I like it too. I know that I could probably never be as beautiful as the models that are usually in makeup ads, but I could have lips like that."

Macy took a few steps towards me so that she could get a better view of the poster, although I am sure she could see it fine from the side. As she did this, my mother's shoes had arrived and she started to try them on.

In a soft sweet voice Macy said to me, "Michelle was right about you, you get it."

I resented the opaqueness of her comment. This woman is researching me like an animal and for her to say I get it, when I clearly don't get it, felt like a menacing taunt. Mom's phone beeped; it received a text. She proceeded to fumble with her phone and talk with the assistant at the same time. Macy nodded her head to the side to follow her to the makeup counter. I followed like a sheep to slaughter. My mom wasn't helping with anything.

Continuing in a light voice, "you don't really wear too much lipstick yet, no?"

"Not really, I mean I wear some lip-gloss."

"But that stuff right there," her hand resting on the counter pointed to some lipstick, "you don't really wear that kind of lipstick yet, huh?"

"No, not really."

"Do you think that is a good price for this brand here?"

I looked at the others. "Well, it's virtually the same as the others, oh, but there is a more expensive one."

"Actually there are three, see, the regular, the ultra, and the premium, all the same brand of lipstick. Of course the packaging for the premium stands out the most."

I nodded.

"Now it doesn't really matter exactly how much money the lipstick is in order to follow this question: only let me tell you this: at this store there are several brands at that price. You won't find anything cheaper, at least not here. Now the ultra is slightly more than other brands here, and, finally, the premium is one of the most expensive anywhere."

"Ok," I was trying to study the other makeup, but everything was a blur and I couldn't really concentrate.

"So my question is: which of the three would you buy, or would you buy a different brand altogether?"

"Well, I don't really have any money and my—"

She spoke over me, "what if money was not that big of an issue?"

"Ok, well, I guess the premium, so long as it's better somehow."

"Oh it is, it lasts longer, has better color, and won't smear when you eat."

"That one then."

"And if you had a job but were not rich?"

I had no idea what she was trying to prove, so I simply said, "the ultra."

"Even though you could do the cheapest here, or even cheaper elsewhere?"

"It depends on how much money I have."

"Fair enough, you see the premium is the stretch, it's the justification for purchasing the ultra. The brand doesn't expect to sell too much of the ridiculously expensive premium. They just offer the premium so that customers can feel good about spending more on the ultra, although the ultra is hardly better than the regular."

My mom called out at us, "ok you two, we should get going. We need to pick up Jimmy."

Macy took down our address and said she would swing by after she got something to eat. My mom bought the heels she was wearing and we left. When we separated from Macy, I completely expected my mom to say something, maybe figure out a way to keep her from coming to the house. I don't think my mom even noticed that Macy left. Voicing my concerns no longer felt like a reasonable option. Only when we got into the car my mom started to notice me again.

"That's a cool job, Elly."

"Yeah."

"What's wrong honey?" She could detect the insincerity in my voice and perhaps some of my worry. I had to make a better effort to be positive in front of her. At this moment, I needed to come up with an excuse for something wrong.

"Oh, ah, you know how Macy said that I have been doing other things for them?"

"Sure."

"Well, I haven't received any feedback on the report I sent in yet."

"Oh don't worry, honey; I am sure it will be fine. So, what did you buy?"

CHAPTER THIRTEEN

Jimmy fell asleep within moments of entering the car. Mom told me he had a good time. I didn't see any of the other monsters when we picked him up this time.

I wanted to tell my mom to make her go away, but I honestly didn't know how at this stage. "Mom, um, don't you think it is getting just a bit late?"

"What do you mean?"

"Like we'll be eating soon?"

"Are you hungry sweetie?"

I really wasn't hungry in the slightest.

"Well, then let's have dinner in about an hour, say eight?"

"Ok, um, but do you think Macy will be still at our house?"

"Oh would you like to have her over for dinner?"

"No. It's just that maybe she shouldn't come over, I mean—"

My mom cut me off, "Elly, we're almost home and I am sure she is not too far off. It's too late now sweetie.

I am sure you are doing fine at your job. She merely wants to go over your stuff. How hard could it be?"

"Ok."

"Just have a snack when we get home."

When we arrived home and pulled into the garage, I thought I saw the silhouette of a woman in a new Honda Accord two houses down. Why would she park so far away? I went to the bathroom to wash up and wake up; my eyes had not gotten any better and my cheeks were starting to break out. Not five minutes had passed since we entered the house did an ominous doorbell ring sound the arrival of Macy.

My mother opened the door for her while I stood in the middle of the hallway, staring through our open-concept living room and kitchen. Around the anteroom wall I could hear, "hello Emily." They both appeared from around the wall smiling. Macy spotted me quickly, "hi Eleanor."

"Hi," she disturbingly chirped in a fresh perky voice. Her appearance seemed just as fresh as when we met that morning. Turning to my mother with her hands folded palm up and palm down, "what a lovely home you have Emily." In our house, her mannerisms took a robotic twist, as if a switch had flipped in her head for a new environment and now she had a new demeanor, yet she still relentlessly pursued knowing everything about me.

"Oh, thank you. We're not finished decorating it, of course."

Macy seemed to take in every square inch of the room, scanning and mentally cataloguing all objects my mom had laid about to decorate it.

"Um, would you like anything to drink Macy?"

"Sure."

"What would you like?"

"Umm…" Macy took a step slowly towards the kitchen; my mom responded in kind. "Would you like to see what we have in the fridge?" I felt compelled to walk over to the kitchen area.

"Sure, I think that would be best." Macy took a glance at the inside of the fridge while Mom started listing off some of the drinks we have, "…and we have some teas and some coffee too."

"Oh, I think I could go for a Tru Blue right about now."

My mom sounded a bit surprised, "ok, here you are."

"Now I have a few things for you to sign. Feel free to take your time to look them over." She had set her purse down on the table and got out the paper work as she spoke, "we'd just like to take an hour or so of Eleanor's time to videotape and see Eleanor's room and bathroom. The video will only be seen by select employees of the *Incantando* agency and none of our clients, although the information we gather, such as clothing color schemes, will become a part of a large database that will be shared with clients of our agency."

My mom sat down and picked up the contract, although I doubt she even read it.

"The videotape will never be sold to anyone else and will be destroyed within two years." Apparently, my mom did read at least one part of the contract. "Wow, another hundred dollars, or was that from earlier today?"

"That's just for right now."

With a big smile my mom looked up at Macy. "Wow! So are you hiring any older girls right now?"

Returning the smile and tone, Macy smiled, "I know huh," and the two of them tilted their heads back and laughed in unison, a contemptuous joint cackle at the luck of youth.

"Well, you guys can take me shopping and go through my closet for a hundred bucks any day."

Macy smiled at her, took a sip of the soda and then smiled at me. My mom had signed and pushed the papers towards me. "Here honey, they need your signature too." I took two stiff steps towards the table and glanced down at the papers; next to my mom's signature was the typed word "Parent/Guardian." "Oh, you don't have to read it honey, just sign it." I looked up at my mom while Macy said, "it's ok, take your time Eleanor."

I couldn't stand to look at Macy, so I focused on the paper. It was about being videotaped. None of the words were "fine print." I should have, theoretically, been able to read every word without a magnifying glass. The occasional bold face sentence stood out like a warning sign for a sharp turn. Regardless, I couldn't really read the words at that instant. I signed.

Macy quickly snatched up the paper, folded it again, and put it back into her purse. "Shall we?" I understood that to mean to go to my room. Mom asked, "should I go with you two?" Macy and I stopped and turned.

"Only if you'd like to…"

"Oh, I think I will put some stuff away and do some accounting."

I started back towards my room with Macy behind me. We left my mom in the kitchen. I could hear Macy going through her purse. Swinging the door open to my room I remembered that I needed to clean it a bit. I ran in and picked up a few things I had laying around. Still on my knees, I looked back at Macy she had a small handheld video camera focused directly on me. The red light on the camera could not have been more obvious. Macy swung it away and started filming my desk as though she hadn't had the camera trained on me for a long time.

I didn't know what to say. So I simply stood up, in the center of my room. I took a glance at the full length mirror. My room wasn't really messy—I usually keep it clean. For some reason I just had trouble keeping it clean at the new house. Often I woke up surprised to find clothes and accessories lying about.

"So maybe we could start with your closet."

I walked towards myself. The red light followed my moves. Then it disappeared as I slid the glass door open.

"So, basically, tell me about your stuff. What's your favorite sweater?"

Without seeing the camera or Macy behind me I felt a little more comfortable. As I picked up the clothes, each fabric felt so distinct at the time. Without searching for it, I suddenly came to my favorite sweater.

"Here, this one."

"Oh how cute! It looks, like, warm too." Macy sounded like one of my girlfriends at our old home.

"Um thanks."

"Now I noticed you checked out a lot of sweaters today but didn't buy any. Could you show me the warm clothing that you have?"

I went through all of my sweaters, light jackets, and jackets while the camera was burning into my back.

"Is there anything that you think you still need to get for winter clothing?"

I turned to see her and the camera was resting along her side in her hand. "Um, well I was searching for like a zip-up hoody today, in a dark color."

"How would that fit in with what you showed me?"

I turned back to the inside of the closet. "Um, like," I started flipping to my hoodies, "like here I have a white one and this one is old and I don't have too many dark colors that are thinner sweaters."

"So would the hoody be in a fabric like this, or like this?"

"Not synthetic, but a soft cotton, or a wool, with, like, a pattern like this one, that would be cool too if I wanted something heavier."

"Oh, I think that would look really good on you." I ventured another look back at the camera, and Macy was filming the closet, and smiling at me. Would I sound like a naïve fool to a dark room full of black suits?

Macy continued in her fake friendly voice, "yeah, I didn't, like, see anything like that today either. So, what kind of shoes would you wear with those sweaters?"

I noticed that my mom had made Macy take off her shoes too. "Um, well I guess those brown outdoorsy flats would be perfect, but," I walked over to the other end of the closet and slid the door open, "but these black ones would work too."

"What do you usually wear with the hoodies you have now?" She was filming the closet again.

"Um, these or these, for the cotton sweater shirts."

"Is the camera bothering you? Would you feel better if I just filmed your clothes and not you? You seem really nervous."

"Um yeah, that would be nice."

"No problem, I will make more of an effort to just get the clothes and stuff. So what about that cute little plaid cap you got today? What would you, like, wear with that?"

I showed her which shoes and which shirts or sweaters I would wear with it. Macy continued to compliment me on all my clothes and choices. Perhaps she had not had enough Tru Blue earlier in the day when she was completely expressionless? When I started talking about my pants, we moved over to my dressers. Macy had me pull out all my pants and show them to the camera. When we finished she asked me, "what about this drawer?"

"That's my underwear drawer."

She waited a moment, staring at me, waiting for an answer to an unasked question. When I didn't do anything she stated, "we don't have to open it."

I started to say something and stopped.

"So what do you need to buy for this drawer?"

"Um, well, I could use some more ankle socks."

"Ok, well, show me your desk area." We walked over and spoke about how much time I spent there, what I did. I didn't mention a diary, although Macy asked if I had one anyways. I said, no. Again, she found ways to give me compliments. Macy checked her watch, "well, would you like to give me a tour of your bathroom?"

We went to the bathroom in the hall. I switched on the light; it was dark outside now. In the mirror I could see Macy standing beside me, her hand keeping the camera focused on the counter.

"Um, I share this with my little brother."

"Oh, how old is he again?"

It was the first time I told her, "he's seven."

"Oh, ok, so how do you two have it organized?"

I pulled out drawers and she filmed the contents. She asked a lot of questions concerning my makeup use: who bought it, how often I could wear it, how often I wanted to wear it, in what situations, how often my mom made exemptions, what punishment if she caught me wearing some when I wasn't supposed to, what I was wearing at that time, what I could get away with, what I felt I needed, what brands I used, why I used those brands. I can't even remember all the questions she asked.

Once she filmed everything she let the camera rest at her side. I had wanted to ask and finally just did it, "so you guys must have a lot to advertise?

"Oh, well, it's not all for us. I mean, we will use everything that we did today, but the advertising department will only use some of it."

"Are you guys getting into the makeup business then?

"Oh, yeah, we have a big client now."

With a breath and without thinking I asked, "so will this be a makeup that does something different than the rest?"

"They do have some market differentiation, but they will be heavily relying on us."

I glanced at the mirror as Macy spoke. She had moved her hand up from her side, and the red light was still on. My body froze. Macy didn't seem that bright, but whoever might be listening to the tape might be.

"I am guessing that you went to the bathroom once you returned home?"

I could only move my mouth, "um… yes."

"Hm, well, do you plan on taking a shower tonight?"

"Yeah."

"Would you mind if I sat in here?"

I didn't move or make a sound.

"While you shower, I wouldn't be filming, or even see you, I would just sit here," she gestured towards the toilet, "and leave once you say you are finished."

"Um, I don't think so, if that's ok?"

"Too weird? Yeah, I think so too, it doesn't hurt to ask. You see we just have this new client who makes shampoo and conditioner and it would help if we knew how people interact with the product…"

"Um, yeah, I'll pass if that's alright?"

"That's totally ok. I think it's weird too," her voice finished in a cheerful crescendo, "but that's my job."

We left the bathroom and Macy headed down the hall toward the front door. My mom was in the kitchen preparing something to eat. Once we got to the living room and within earshot of my mom, Macy turned around, "thank you so much for showing me around tonight, Eleanor."

In a light voice I responded, "you're welcome."

"Really it was very nice of you. You have excellent taste and some really cool stuff."

"Thanks."

Macy went over towards my mom while I stayed back at the mouth of the hallway, exhausted. They went back and forth. Macy seemed to be full of compliments. Finally, Macy headed for the door. In my room I started thinking about all the homework I had due. The doorbell rang. My mom had seemed busy with dinner so I went to get the door, but my mom had already got to the door. Now she and Macy were in the kitchen.

"I know it seems silly to buy water in a plastic bottle when you're out at lunch, but this one has healthy minerals."

"Mm," my mom went for two glasses. A large glass bottle, apparently mineral water, rested on the table.

"Watch, give it a year and all those sandwich chains will be serving the same mineral water." Macy twisted the top and I could hear the seal break from the shadow of the hallway. "It's really popular in Europe."

I had every opportunity to stop Mom from drinking that "mineral" water from Macy, but somehow I didn't care. It was only going to be a matter of time. My mother took a sip, said something intelligible to Macy, who encouraged her to drink more. She did.

With a genuine smile, Macy said, "you'll have to have Eleanor tell me what you think. I really must be going"

"Ok, thank you so much for the mineral water."

"Don't mention it, like I said, I just thought of you two while I was at the store and, hey, it would be nice to get one for you to try."

That night I did some more research online. I investigated secret societies a lot more: Illuminati, Freemasons, Skull and Bones, the Bilderberg Group, the Priory of Sion, Opus Dei, etc... This was something I had been doing for some time. I would not call it an obsession; I just spent an inordinate amount of time researching these groups. That's "normal" right? Reading about just one of these societies is gripping. Historical events are explained completely differently than they are in school. Individuals with connections in secret societies are the "movers-and-shakers" of worldwide events.

I wanted to find a historical connection with the virus/spell. I had a dual theory: one for the virus and one for witches—which I had a hard time reconciling. The narrative I constructed in my mind, for the virus, needed some confirming evidence.

The general narrative is: the virus arrived at some point in history, infecting very few at first. So if the point in history is WWII, then the Bilderberg Group in Europe or the Skull and Bones in Northeast America are the virus societies. If the point in history is the medieval era or the Dark Ages, then the Illuminati or Opus Dei, both in Italy, are the initial virus societies.

Only a few are infected, maybe a hundred or less, I don't know exactly, but the point is the virus has a lot of trouble spreading because of bad transmission or whatever. The infected people are just average people in society at first. However, with superior intellect from the virus, powers to manipulate and a singular blunt purpose, those very few infected rose to positions of power and formed secret societies where they could get close enough to ensure infections of new members. Many of the secret societies drink from communal chalices... Maybe they experimented with different virus concoctions until they finally found an effective recipe with Tru Blue?

Despite the small numbers, the society became strong and influential. They decided which paths countries would take and always covered their tracks. Now they are growing in numbers and making final preparations for massive infections by observing people like me for information.

So there is one, like, humongous, problem with this little narrative: the members of the secret societies were always men. And many women are involved now, and the men, not so much. And then the whole witch thing, I cannot get that straight in my mind. It's not just the class project about witch burning, although I had been thinking about the curse I need to create.

What is the difference between witch trials as opposed to mob justice of male political figures? Were burned witches simply women infected by the virus who had betrayed the virus' cause? The witches were rebelling viruses? That doesn't make sense.

More fundamentally, what is a witch? What is a curse from a witch? A curse from a witch is a method of one person manipulating another person. I suppose the secret male societies could be warlocks, those are male witches. And I suppose when *Incantando* uses the word, "virus" they really mean "curse." The more I read about secret societies, the more my proposed narrative didn't add up.

I went to my room and held my windowsill elephant. She had been carved asymmetrically; one side of her had more details than the other. I wondered who carved her and who painted her. More importantly, should she gaze out the window at the stars, or gaze inward? Is the curse out of my control? Are witches out of my control?

If the elephant gazes inwards, I have control, and then the secret societies are witches. All I would have to do is *expose* them. I could simply show the world that a definite and secret group of powerful individuals are really controlling things. Once they are exposed, human beings will rise up and take back control. I don't have to battle all the witches, mere exposure is enough.

Or, alternatively, and better yet, maybe the secret societies are not all that bad. Sure, a few witches controlling the world seems, just plain bad, but if they did good things? Wouldn't that be wonderful? That's what the world needs, impartial and highly intelligent "beings" fixing the world's problems. All I have to do is convince a few of the witches that everyone will be better off if they use their powers for the common good.

And then I turned the elephant outward, meaning I have no control, and I got confused, and I felt a little frightened. What if there were no witches attacking our society, infecting us, cursing us? I couldn't really answer that question. I had been so obsessed the last few days and now confusion flooded my entire body. Everything I had been thinking was completely and utterly wrong. What if there were no secret societies controlling the world? My confusion grew and I started to cry. I didn't know why I was crying, which only made me feel worse. How come people would deliberately burn a woman to death? How come Macy wanted to film all of my clothes and stuff? Why are my parents getting a divorce, because my mom had money from her job? How come when I try to make new friends at school, the first thing the girls do is look me up and down? How come *Incantando* uses the word virus and straps cords to little boys while they watch television? And if the secret societies are not in control, does that not also mean other leaders have no control? What if all the political, cultural, academic leaders are really powerless to effect change? I sat in horror, crying. No one is in control and the world is adrift in hate, isolated amongst slowly dying suns.

CHAPTER FOURTEEN

The next morning I woke up with a headache. At least I hadn't had any bad dreams. I seemed to have slept through the whole night. After locking the bathroom door behind me, I went for the cabinet that had aspirin. With my outstretched hand paused in mid-air, the evening before came back to me—the camera, the red light, Macy flipping or twisting everything in the bathroom to show the camera the labels—and I decided not to ingest any aspirin.

Opening the front door to check the weather, it felt similar to the day before. The temperature was slightly cooler, but then again I got up much later on Sunday. The sky was clear and it promised to be a moderate autumn day. Nothing cheered me up though. My mom almost made me late once again.

Once I entered Mr. Sword's classroom, I could feel his eyes watching me. He was probably watching me through the window. We were supposed to work with our presentation groups the first thirty minutes of class. Mr. S.

decided against anything more than ten minutes though, because so many students were absent. His only remark was deliberately banal, "it's flu season again." Sure, flu season, or maybe Tru Blue is taking hold. Mark was there, but Rob was absent again.

"You work on the project at all this weekend?"

"No."

"Me neither."

Mark didn't look normal or natural compared to our peers. He appeared alert, reserved, and contemplative. I wanted to get one good long look at him, search his face like searching for silhouettes on the moon, before I risked a direct question I had wanted to ask. I caught his eyes; he accepted and turned his head to look directly at me. He gave me a smile as if to ask, "what is it?"

"Mark, um, have you like drank any of that new soda?"

"Tru Blue?" I could already tell that he hadn't. "No, you kind of freaked me out."

I might have been blushing. "Oh, sorry about that, it's just that, um, well Rob's house has exactly the same layout as my new house, and I didn't really notice it until Rob brought those sodas over and then I remembered the time and everything."

"Oh, it's alright, it's cool, you know last Friday, they put some of it in the machines?"

I didn't know that. I mistrusted most of my peers, now I truly could not trust anyone.

"Yep, but word is that they might have to take it out soon, all of the soda, like tomorrow."

"Why's that?"

"Some parent group is forcing them to do it."

"Oh." Was there some hope left?

He gave me a knowing smile. "Have you tried it?"

"No. Um, it's the fake sugar, I don't really drink soda." I had done some research on the net for some excuses, "It's basically like liquid candy." I thought of other excuses to appear natural: the environmental impact of aluminum mining, a product made abroad in water scarce third-world countries, or unlivable cheap wages to employees. Health was a good reason, since soda is a food item, and people don't really understand fake sugar.

"Oh, yeah, it's probably not good for you to drink it." His reply seemed to have an understanding in it.

He then picked up on what I said about Rob's house, "Yeah, those houses are strange over there. So that's where you live, huh?"

"Yep."

"I mow lawns in that subdivision; I don't live too far from Rob's. It is a long walk though, especially when you're pushing a mower."

"That's cool. So is that your summer job or something."

"Yeah, it's really strange all the houses kinda look the same, I have to keep a record book of all the addresses and their phone numbers. I wish I could get a bunch of customers next to each other and then I could push the mower straight all the way down the block. I'm surprised you haven't heard of my lawn cutting business."

"Why," I paused, "should I?"

"Well, I used to do this thing. Well, I still kinda do. I used to cut that vodka bottle shape into people's lawn." He outlined the top of the bottle with his finger on the desk.

"You know, like cut all the grass around the bottle so

the tall uncut grass sticks out as a darker taller green. I would even spell out the name with the dead grass. They used to pay me five dollars for each picture with the bottle and a different address. I was supposed to ask the owners if they wanted to keep it for a brief period of time and volunteer to cut it a few days later."

"Oh that's a cool job, I guess. Do you *drink*?"

"No, that's part of the reason I stopped doing it. My mom found out and was pissed. My parents are divorced and my dad kinda drinks a lot. I don't think I will ever drink. I only did it for the money. Eventually, I didn't even ask the owners of the lawns if they wanted to keep it since they never wanted to keep it. I'd just take the picture."

"Oh, I am sorry to hear that." I hesitated and couldn't help but glance down at my desk, "my parents are splitting up."

"Em, I'm sorry to hear that. You know it's not that bad, so long as your father isn't a dick. I have other friends whose parents are divorced and it's cool."

"Yeah, me too."

"Honestly, like don't worry about it. It's out of your control, you know what I mean."

"Sure." I wanted to change the tone of the conversation a bit, "so, um, you think my neighbors would have heard of the vodka lawnmower?"

"Ha, no, that's not the reason. When my mom made me stop, I contemplated cutting," he spoke in a silly voice, "that famous soda bottle." He seemed a bit embarrassed and went back to talking normal, "you know that hourglass shape," he traced his fingers on the desk again, "but I never received any replies to my emails. So I started cutting my own shapes, my technique was really good by then, I understood how the shapes would be viewed from further away, like the front door, and I would adjust the height of the blades, and everything. Some customers were keeping them for a few days to show friends and stuff. So when I did get a reply to my emails, and it was even for more money, I said screw them, people actually want to keep my designs."

Was he speaking in code? "Cool, do you, um, still take pictures?"

"Yeah."

"Could I get your Facebook address?"

"Oh I don't put them on there. This is kinda, you know, underground. Here's my Facebook name though. I could email you some pictures." He was speaking in code.

"Yeah, that would be cool; I'd like to see some."

The bell rang. What a loud and excessive noise it was too. I had to go outside to get to the next classroom; the sun hit my face and I felt warmth for the first time in days. I closed my eyes, tilted my head back, and took it in. At the time I wasn't completely sure, but why not, why couldn't Mark be a part of some resistance? Or maybe he had some suspicion and knew of an organization based on the net?

That night I called up Jamie. "Eleanor, I'm so happy to hear from you. I'm sorry I didn't call this weekend. I was out of town and, like, you won't believe it, but I left my cell phone at home."

"Oh, that's ok Jamie. I was busy this weekend too."

"So, how's, like, everything going?"

"Oh you know," at this point I couldn't trust anyone. "How are you doing?" Jamie started telling me about her trip, how school was going, etc… Nothing was unusual.

"I was wondering if you have Darcy's number. I haven't been able to find her online and I know that both of your parents are friends."

"Ah, yeah, sure. Just let me get my mom's phonebook. It's going to be her home phone."

"That's fine."

After a reasonable amount of time, Jamie read the phone number to me. She didn't ask why I wanted Darcy's number and we chitchatted some more. As soon as we said goodbye, I gave Darcy's house a call. She answered the phone. From her greeting, I could tell she was surprised and delighted.

"It's so good to hear from you. I thought about calling. I spoke with Ariel the other day and she said you were doing alright." I could not hear any sense of hidden meaning in her voice.

"Yeah, so how have you been?"

"Oh, you know, the same." This seemed to be something of a hint.

"That's good to hear."

"So, how is, like, your new school and everything?"

"Um, it's cool, pretty much the same really, except it is filled with people I don't know yet." I kept going because she seemed to be interjecting every chance she got. "So I was, like, thinking, the other day, about your brother, and figured I'd give you a call."

"Oh," all sound of happiness faded in her voice.

"You know I always used to speak with him when I came over to your house and I started thinking about him again." I was rambling. Perhaps I should have thought out my speech more. Darcy and I used to be close friends around five years ago, but we drifted apart. We just didn't have the same interest. I didn't want to make it sound as if she still wasn't my friend though.

"Um, well, I guess you wouldn't have heard since you were moving and everything, but Malcolm died a few days before you moved."

"Oh! I am so sorry to hear that! I didn't know…"

"We didn't talk too much about it. The funeral was out of state and mostly family."

"I'm so sorry about your brother."

"Thanks."

"How are you doing?"

"Oh, I'm hanging in there."

The phone went silent for a bit as I tried to figure out what it all meant. I wasn't going to be deterred though. Malcolm was on to them and I needed to find out whatever information I could. "Where was the funeral held?"

"Oh, you know how I told you about my grandma's cottage?"

"Sure,"

"Well we went up there."

"Um, how did he die?"

She took a deep breath, but said nothing. After another pause she began, "Eleanor, well, you know that he was sick, you know, mentally sick?"

"Yes…" I wanted to mention some of his behavior and more importantly his comments about water bottles, but I decided to let her finish. Who knows if she could be trusted?

"Well, he was institutionalized a second time and Dad went to visit him and took him out for lunch since the doctors had spoken about maybe having him return home."

Silence once again filled the phone. I couldn't hear if she was crying or not. I knew I would have to wait though.

"Elly," when Darcy and I were friends, "Elly" was what I liked to be called, "you know I trust you, and I have always thought that you were one of the sweetest persons I know."

"Thanks Darcy."

"I'm completely serious; you have always been so nice to me and everyone else around you. I couldn't say that for most people at our school."

"Of course I have always been nice to you."

"Yeah, but I know we haven't really been close friends or anything for a few years now, since we were little kids. Just promise me. Promise me you won't tell anyone."

"Sure."

How come she trusted me so much? Perhaps she knows of a way to tell when someone is infected? Or, the more likely reason: she just didn't know.

She took another heavy breath. "Well after lunch my father went to the bathroom. He sometimes gets stomach trouble… And when he finally came back out Malcolm had been hit by a semi-truck on the highway near the diner."

"Oh my, someone hit him?"

"You know he had issues. He was a paranoid schizophrenic, Eleanor."

I wasn't sure what to say so I said quietly, "I know."

"It actually wasn't clear if he ran in front of the truck or if the truck hit him pulling off the highway, because I guess there's something of an off-ramp there. But no one saw the accident and the highway patrol studied the skid marks and concluded that it wasn't the truckers fault. Although I overheard my father talking with an attorney, and the attorney said it still may have been the truckers fault, but we could only recover for our families mental pain and suffering since my brother's future earnings would not have been much on account of the mental diagnosis, isn't that an awful thing to say?"

"That is terrible, the whole thing, I'm so sorry Darcy. Is there anything I can do?"

Darcy hesitated. I could picture her with a phone to her ear, sitting on her bed staring out the window at the backyard we used to play in. Would she let me know what to do?

"No."

That was the end of the conversation. We gave each other goodbyes and promises to stay in touch. As for any help in battling Malcolm's demons, the time had already passed.

For the first time I had a mortal fear—I might die. Up until then, my fear was more nebulous, like a dark toxic fog, one that would forever change me into something else, something not just placid, mindless, and controlled, but hurtful. I read once that early coal miners, those that had to use flamed lamps, pickaxes and shovels, had various names for the toxic colorless gases. Day after day, miners would see a cold morning sun for a few brief moments on the path to work. Then they crawled in dark coal mines to swing axes at supporting walls and shovel dirty and dusty black coal into heavy carts, hand-pushed to the light coming from the surface. And what did they call the numerous toxic gases? Damps. Firedamp was explosive gases which could potentially engulf the men in a fiery inferno. Stink damp was some gas with sulfur, which reeked of spoiled eggs. Blackdamp and Whitedamp were different gases, but similar in the deadly sense that the gas could asphyxiate the miners. Incidentally, these asphyxiating damps are why miners brought canaries to constantly tweet in the mine—only in the birds' silent death would the warning be heard.

A horrifying damp noiselessly and colorlessly settling over everyone I knew was terrible enough, yet I always felt it could be undone. Venoms have antidotes; bacteria have antibiotics and antibodies; viruses have antivirals, antibodies, and vaccinations; curses have cures and counter-curses; but death…has no return.

The witches arranging the murder of Malcolm gave me more perspective on their ambitions. Malcolm certainly had issues, although his rants occurred infrequently, his beliefs made him largely dysfunctional in society, and yet he never harmed anyone—quite the opposite. His interactions with me and others had a simple and constant kindness. He didn't have a hero's birth, nor did he live a hero's life, yet he performed incalculably diffusive acts, strictly unhistorical, which contributed to the mounting good in the world.

CHAPTER FIFTEEN

DATE: _____

They have been here for some time. Perhaps they tried a massive infection of curse before, but they failed for whatever reason. Perhaps that was some plague in history. Perhaps Malcolm heard of the attempted curses through bottled water and they murdered him. Perhaps using regular water tasted funny with the curse in it, so now they are using soda and mineral water. They are trying other things.

A Virus can stand-by watching and let the person, the "host," continue to go about their day until it has a really important reason to take control, such as drinking more Tru Blue to refresh or become stronger.

- What I can do -

Not drink soda or other Virus/curse products — when people ask, I say — it's unhealthy, it's harmful to the environment, it's negative/harmful to other people/workers.

1) Write about it, explain to others.
2) Tell people negative things about Tru Blue — too risky!
3) Show people negative/harmful things concerning Tru Blue — too risky?
4) Research how the Virus/curse works.
5) Find other people that know.

CHAPTER SIXTEEN

The next day at school I needed to do something; I wasn't going to simply give up despite the appearance of any effort being futile. Mark mentioned that they might be removing the soda from the school; I might be able to find out something in regards to the distribution of it. At the time, I even contemplated sneaking into the truck.

I also needed to make a move on Mark. The day before, everything surrounding our conversation was covert, nothing explicit, only innuendo, hints, and implicit understandings. The setting is what really threw things off. I needed to get Mark out of the school away from our spellbound peers.

For the second straight day many students were missing from school. That morning in history Mr. S. gave us time to prepare our group presentations. Again I moved to Mark and Rob since they were already sitting together and conversing.

"Wait so what happened, I don't think I get what you're complaining about."

"Ok, so the goalie had the puck covered on the ice in his glove hand. His glove webbing is made of mesh, and when they reviewed the play, anyone could see through the webbing that the puck had crossed the goal-line."

"So what's your complaint again?"

"The ref didn't notice it in the review. It was a goal dude, but only the announcers noticed it in their video replay."

"Oh, that's a bummer for your team, man."

I chimed in, "you know, people used to wear mesh shirts in the 80's until it went out of style. Maybe the goalie should change his glove style."

"Ha, yeah totally, get a solid web."

"Yeah, but isn't that dishonest, I mean the puck did cross the line."

"But dude, they could install sensors in the puck and the ice if they wanted too."

"I doubt it, the league took forever to get instant replay after football was doing it."

"I don't know, man, I can barely watch a football game with all the reviews."

"It's what people want, man, I mean, there's nothing worse than a bad call for your team. It's an honest game."

"No it's not. I've seen plenty of bogus pass interference calls, or non-calls."

"Hey, get to work you two!" Mr. S. called out from the desk.

Rob moved slower than usual. His round eyes had round bags beneath them. "Hey sorry for not being here yesterday. I was so tired. I slept for an incredible amount of time. What did I miss?"

"Oh not too much, man. We only got a few more pages

done in the book."

"And we had some time to work on our presentation, but Mark and I agreed to think more about it after class."

Mark sat up straight. "Ok, so for the witch burning skit, we're going to use one of the janitor's brooms for the post and some of our history books for the wood to set afire. What about you, Eleanor?"

"I was thinking you'd hold my wrist behind my back and we would both walk over to the pole."

"And then I act like I tied your hands to the pole or should we get some cloth?"

"I think it will be fine for me to grip it since it will be behind me and away from the class anyways. I think I'll probably struggle a bit, so hold me tight." Mark blushed a bit. I couldn't believe it and might have blushed a little myself. "I have to figure out what to say still."

Rob finally showed some sign of life, "Whoa, you don't know what you're gonna say yet?"

"Well, I don't think it's all that important. The important thing is how we interact." I smiled at Mark.

Mark quickly regained his composure from the thoughts of gripping me tight. "Yeah, but we got to come up with something cool." All of us paused in reflection. Nothing seemed too different with Rob, only a new sleepiness and sluggishness instead of his normal calm.

Mark must have slouched again because he sat up straight. "I got it, what's the worse curse you guys could think of?"

We paused again for a moment. Rob seemed to have awakened from his sleep. "How about you curse everyone so their sexual parts fall off?"

Mark gave a loud long, "Ohhhh…"

"Yeah, like everyone's junk just like rots and totally falls off."

"Ye-ah," I wanted to change the tact of the conversation. "You know I was thinking at the beginning of the curse I would say that burning me alive is a prerequisite for me giving the curse. You know, like my burnt body is the last part of the potion to make the curse happen."

"Perfect. For the curse, I was thinking like, maybe everyone has to feel your pain. You know, like they experience being burnt alive too; except that they have to live with the feeling of being burnt alive for the rest of their lives, if they can take it."

"That's a good idea too. Hey I gotta take a leak, I'll be right back."

Mark and I were silent until Rob left the room completely. "I don't know," Mark started to turn a little red as he spoke, "I think the worse curse might be the inability to experience, you know," he looked at the floor, "like powerful emotions and stuff." I felt safe exploring every aspect on his gorgeous face because I knew he wasn't going to stop looking at the floor. He had long eyelashes, which really highlighted his brilliant steely cobalt blue eyes. Mark continued, "like, if you couldn't experience love for another person."

I paused. I didn't know what to say, yet I had to say something. "Is that the curse you think that I should put on the class?"

He hesitated, "no, I just think it's the worse curse you could say."

"So what do you think I should say?"

Now he was staring at the ceiling with his lower lip

tucked under his upper teeth. Finally he turned to me and said, "you could tell everyone that they will have to live with the *doubt* that they were wrong. That you were not a witch, but the curse will still haunt them for the rest of their lives because they killed an innocent person."

"Is doubt really that bad?"

"No, but people don't like to punish people unless they are sure that person deserves it."

"I suppose. My dad always says that uncertainty paralyzes."

"What does that mean?"

"I'm not sure, but I think doubt and uncertainty are pretty much the same thing." We paused for an instant together, before I had the courage to ask him the question, "so you don't believe they were really witches?"

"Come on; are you serious? Like some weird lady actually gave a teenage girl some pimples or bad breath, or something stupid like that?"

What I wanted to say was, "yes, absolutely, that is what they did and what they are doing." Of course, I couldn't be so blunt. I wasn't sure how to approach this; I definitely didn't want my demeanor to give anything away. I tried to speak in as natural a voice as possible, not in a whisper or too excited. "Couldn't the witches, you know, be more ambitious? I mean, they're always portrayed as menacing, vindictive, evil women, but what if the truth was different? What if the covens are more organized and they want to control everyone, running experiments and studying people for the ultimate curse of control?"

He looked at me softly and not too closely, "I never thought of that one." He remained silent looking at the ground again. He glanced up at me, "why would they do that though?"

"Why wouldn't witches have grand plans?"

He sat back in his chair as if quizzing me, "and the ultimate spell would be... what?"

Mark acted like he was considering the conversation as a thought-experiment, although he probably had nothing to say and wanted me to make the next comment. Finally, I broke the silence and coolly asked, "the thing that gets me is: why wouldn't they do something when they were burned alive?"

"Maybe they had grander plans, like what you said," Mark gave me a smile. "Maybe they need to be burnt alive as part of the ultimate curse, as you say."

Suddenly in the corner of my eye, I caught Rob's bulky silhouette.

"Hey Rob!"

"Sorry to interrupt, but I heard the end of what you were saying," he stopped speaking as he fit into his seat, "but all I heard was 'need to be burnt' and it totally reminded me."

I was surprised he heard that much as he was so far away, and I tried to remember exactly what we said before he came back.

"So, I was reading about your part of the presentation Eleanor, and I came across this webpage that was really good. I don't think we could steal it, but I forgot to save it anyway."

"What is it man? Out with it."

"Alright, just chill... so, in the colonial era we only punished the 'body,' right?" He made the quotation marks with his fingers. "Burning, hanging, branding, flogging, the stocks, whipping: all of that punished the 'body.' It was just *pain*, right? But nowadays we, like, reform people, we try and like change their minds. We try to make them all like responsible and stuff."

Mark interjected, "I read something about that. Burning is to purify the body because purity was important to accomplish before death."

"Wait, wait, so the other thing is, like, really trippy. They didn't really have liberty back then, I mean, not like what we think of liberty today. They sort of like invented it with the Constitution and everything, you know—life, liberty, and the pursuit of happiness. So it wouldn't have made sense to lock people up before that, because locking people up is all about taking away liberty."

I felt more comfortable from the initial shock of Rob returning so quickly. "That's interesting Rob, but they did have jails. I have done some research."

"Yeah, but they were only temporary right? They temporarily locked people up for a few days before the hanging or until the stocks were vacant."

"Yeah, I think I read that. There was something like only one real prison, and that wasn't even used for all the colonies."

Mr. S.'s voice came booming from the corner of the room, "alright, if you haven't finished, you need to work on it some other time, but not during other peoples' presentations. I want you to think about the historical comparisons of other groups. There will be a quiz once we are finished with all of them."

A collective noise of displeasure arose from our peers punctuated by a few muffled swear words. I never thought of the question until then, but I raised my hand without giving it another thought. "Do you mean modern-day comparisons, for us tenth graders or Americans in general?"

"Excellent question Eleanor, ah, either." I pressed Rob for his ideas of historical comparisons for our group's topic. "So what do you think *liberty* means today exactly, besides not being locked up?"

"Well, being able to live and work where you want?"

"I mean, you though, what does liberty mean specifically to you? You don't work, but you have to go to school, don't you?"

"Yeah, but, well…"

Mark was ready. "We still get to choose who our friends are."

Rob found an answer that none of us could argue with, "well to a certain extent, I mean none us are buying Ferraris, but we still have a lot of choices of what to buy."

•   •   •

At break, I began my search for the location of all the drink machines. I didn't see anything unusual during the first break. Only a handful of my classmates bought some sodas, but it was still early in the day. I was sure there'd be more.

During lunch break I finally saw the delivery truck. Two men wearing navy Dickies and shirts with cloth badges went from machine to machine. Instead of an empty dolly to cart the soda away, the dolly was filled with bottled juice. They were removing the soda, and replacing it with sealed juice…

During the break between the second-to-last and last class, I caught a glimpse of the man from *Incantando*. He wore a shirt and tie. I couldn't make a closer observation because of time constraints, but I made up my mind to find him before the last class got out.

. . .

After the police left that night, I reread the journal entry about the man chasing me. Funny how I had noted the shapes cut into lawns while jogging home after being chased. They won't be there now though: nothing lasts. Not even doves kissing from two different lawns. One would be gone and the other would soon fly away too. The birthday cake would have been blown out, eaten and forgotten. The smiley face would change expression and be cut away from the world. Did the smiley face have two bushes as bundles of hair on its head? Was it someone's birthday? Did two neighbors finally stop feuding? Did they ask Mark or did he already know the situation? For the first time in days I felt hope; I didn't recall seeing any bottles of vodka or soda.

During the night I gently woke absorbed in anxiety about Mark's lawn art, as if I missed something of paramount importance. Too alert to fall back asleep, I sat up and rested my feet on the floor and fought the compulsion to go outside and inspect the lawns for clues that could only make sense at that very moment. Why not? I dressed and slowly walked through the house and quietly cracked the front door. The night air produced more certainty, compelling me to find a definitive sign, firm evidence about the mystery of the witches, whom I could feel some distance away, asleep or preoccupied.

Outside, the air and even the streetlights felt crisp. All

the lawns looked identical, typical and plain. And then I saw a symbol—formed by the uncut grass around it—a familiar yet unrecognizable pictogram, a childish exercise, but from Mark it had some charm. Although I didn't recognize the symbol, it was still filled with meaning. I didn't stop because I could vaguely see another insignia the next yard over. Again, extremely familiar, the word for the emblem on the tip of my tongue, although this emblem meant more than a word, it had a story, one that I felt, more than I knew: safety, commitment, and the trust of a protective uncle, always looking out for you. A loud humming arose from the houses or the streetlights, and for whatever reason, I just ignored it, as if it were merely the hum of a television. Walking down the dark isolate street, I saw more emblems, each with a vague narrative and distinct feel: fuzzy, warm, playful; and, dark, powerful, confident…

In the dark I heard Ariel's voice, "Eleanor, where are you?"

Shocked and excited I called back to her, "Ariel, what are you doing out here?"

"Looking for you."

She stood across the street looking around, lost and worried, but not worried about herself.

"I'm right here."

Yet she still searched around, walking slowly and slightly craning her neck, not like she was blind, but as if she was surrounded by darkness.

"Ariel! Hey, I'm right here."

"You sound so strange."

I crossed the street towards her and she intently searched in my general direction.

"Elly, is it you?

"Of course."

And once I was only a few steps away, all the features of her face drooped in terror, and without even a scream she turned around and ran as fast as she could.

CHAPTER SEVENTEEN

The dream from the prior night repeatedly interrupted my thoughts throughout the day. I would interpret it one way, satisfactorily, and only an hour later I would come up with another explanation. Most disturbingly, in the morning I found a lot of my stuff and clothes randomly thrown around my room and the bathroom, probably because I had been sleepwalking.

Early in the morning, I briefly spoke with Mark. Many people were still missing from class. I needed to speak with Mark alone so I hurried out of history and waited until he walked out.

"Hey Eleanor," he kept walking in the same direction.

"I need to speak with you." I casually started walking with him.

"Ok," he slowed down a bit, but nothing too noticeable.

"Do you still have basketball practice at four?"

"Yeah."

"Let's meet at the Burger King right after school then."

Now he slowed down more, which must have appeared a bit odd, so I kept the same pace. He started walking faster again. "Ok, so right after school."

"Yep," I veered off and walked towards my class.

The morning was brisk and the afternoon proved to be no better. A deep exhale was clearly visible. I headed straight to our meeting place as soon as the bell rang. Mark arrived a few minutes later; he must have been speaking with some friends, smart.

I had asked for a glass of water and drank from the plastic cup as Mark came in the burger place. He slid into his seat and dropped his bag on the floor with a thud. Since I asked him there, I felt a little obligated to ask him, "would you like anything to eat or drink?" My voice felt slightly quieter than usual.

"No, ha, I was surprised you'd like a fast food place. You know, it's very unhealthy." I knew about the cameras and that most of the employees had probably been spellbound, but I had chosen a distant spot, and no microphones would be planted in such a mundane place.

I had to let him know that I was legitimate. "Mark, I am not sure about their origins, but I know they are on to something big."

He started laughing. After three or four seconds he looked straight at me, "What are you talking about?"

"You know, yesterday how we spoke about the project?"

He smiled, now he kept his voice down, "you know I thought that was, like, extremely creative."

"Thanks," I had thought about how to go about talking with Mark, "yeah, you know I think we stumbled onto some real history with the witch burning."

"Yeah, me too, it's really interesting. So is that what you wanted to talk about."

I leaned towards him a bit and articulated, "yes."

"Oh ok, well what have you got?"

"Well, nothing really, but I want to help. I want to do something but I just don't know anyone."

Mark gave me a weird look. "Well you know, you really don't have to put a curse on the class. I was thinking we could do a video instead. Trust me, teachers love'em. I've actually done it before. We have this editing program on our computer, and it would only take like a few hours. This is funny because I had been thinking that we could make a film."

"And then what?"

His eyebrows curled in confusion.

"Or do you think we could put it on YouTube?"

He was smiling again, "yeah, we could, no problem." He leaned back in his seat. "You know, you are really weird, just like red said."

"The redhead?!"

"Yeah."

"What did she say?"

He smirked again, it was cute, but I felt so uncomfortable now. "Well, she was saying that you had lunch with her and some friends one day. Emily brought you over."

I shook my head slowly, remembering.

"And after everyone finished their lunch, you stayed at the table and she came back to tell you something, and there you were writing down, like, descriptions of their clothing, and, like, what they said and stuff."

Although all my muscles tightened as he spoke, my face didn't feel hot. My expression did not move. I had developed an excellent poker face. "Mark, I should probably tell you this, since I don't have anyone else. I work for an advertising agency called *Incantando*. I do, like, undercover research for them. I tell them what people are wearing, buying, talking about, whatever I think is cool at the moment."

"Oh," his face shifted in series of really perplexing looks, "that's cool, I guess."

"Mark, they are with Tru Blue."

He tossed his head back and gave a quick laugh, "your favorite soda!"

Was he putting on a show now, for the camera? "Mark, I work with someone really high up. Her name is Michelle Mayer. You can like tell from the others that she is the boss around there. She flies all around the country for her job."

Mark bobbed his head with a tight lipped smile-frown on his face. "Do you get paid?"

"Yeah," I went to my bag for my phone, "they gave me this."

"Whoa! This can do like *anything*!"

"Yeah I know."

Mark smiled at me. "Can I see it?"

I handed it to him. He looked at it in delight. "Do you mind if I flip through your apps and stuff."

"Go for it."

"All I got on my old school phone is a camera. Well, I got a voice recorder, which I use sometimes to get-down cool ideas I have sometimes." He kept his head down flipping through my phone's features.

As soon as the thought came to me I was already asking Mark, "could I email a video?"

"Of course."

"What about, like, automatically?"

"What do you mean?"

"Like, take a voice recording, or video, and I have my camera, email it to someone, say, at seven o'clock on its own."

"I don't see why not. If your phone can't do that already I am sure you could find an app on the internet that would do that for you."

We both remained silent. Mark handed back my phone, "that's pretty sweet."

"Ok, I think I see what to do now."

"Cool. I think it'll be the coolest video I've ever made."

"What exactly do you think I should say though?"

"Just what you told me two days ago, about how witches have world domination plans, well, I guess you could say something like, you're working on the ultimate curse."

"Ok."

Mark got excited now, "and you can tell everyone, that, oh, I could get some stock video of like a colonial mob yelling, and I'll shoot you with only blue sky in the background."

"Ok, but it wouldn't make a lot of sense to have one of the witches say all of their secrets," I drew a deep breath and continued, "unless, the person was in the process of being transformed into a witch." I already knew this truth, the Agency had been changing me, but speaking it out loud to Mark made it feel imminent and I had to close my eyes for a moment.

"Hmm, yeah, we'll have to think about that one. When do you want to film? I have a tournament this weekend. But I don't have practice tomorrow and I would have to edit it by Friday."

"I could do it tomorrow, but what about Rob?"

"Oh, I'm sure he's not busy."

"But what am I going to say?"

Mark smiled. "We shouldn't tell him what you're saying until we start filming. He'll be like, 'what the…!?'"

Mark had to get ready for practice so I walked to the elementary school, picked up Jimmy, and went home. I had to think about the video more. Mark could probably put the date at the beginning in white letters to establish the setting. I found some nasty old brown clothes and a brown sack. I cut them up a bit; they seemed decent. The real problem was a probable speech and what kind of liquid the witches would have used to cast their spell on colonial Americans.

Surely they thought of every which way to curse us. Food and water had to be a first choice. I went into our kitchen and opened the fridge, then peeked in the cupboards. For some reason, I recalled Tehching and his journal in the modern art museum. He definitely would have to lock himself up to see no art for a year. Every food, every product, even the leftover containers were artistic. The stuff under the sink, the appliances, even some of my clothes. Of course, they didn't have most of this stuff in the colonial era… no bright green sparkling dishwashing soap containers, let alone dishwashers, but they still managed to wash dishes.

When I went into my bathroom, I had even less to

work with. They probably didn't have shampoo and conditioner. And anti-acne wipes didn't exist. Mark thought that pimples existed in the colonial era. He had said that witches didn't exist, rather people blamed others, as witches, for their faces breaking out. Were people hideous back then? Did anyone really care about breakouts, or split-ends, or is that just a modern worry?

Eventually, I gave up searching for vectors of spells and I took a note pad to write down some lines for the film:

> You won't even know for sure if you're cursed. From _inside_ of you we watch others and yourself. Only when we have reason to control you, do we take control, like when we need you to put more of the curse into or onto your body.

My mom finally came home around six. She was upset about something; I assumed it was in regards to Dad. But I was wrong; it was her new boss at work. Mom had said that she liked her job. Yet if I kept asking why she liked her job, it became clear she didn't. Then the idea struck me: why not a disgruntled witch researcher in colonial America? The witch coven decides not to rescue her and she won't escape the burning, so she confesses all.

Both Jamie and Ariel called. I felt a little bad for ignoring them. I couldn't trust them, so I pretended that everything was fine. Something was different though. I know now that it was me. I lost something that night.

CHAPTER EIGHTEEN

The first thing anyone would notice about Mark's house is that he has no lawn. Instead, the front of the house is shaded with beech trees; the vine-like-branches cover the pale white trunks scarred with black bark. The house was charming and surprising. You simply wouldn't expect a lawn artist to have no front lawn at his house. I didn't spend much time inside the house, but it was older, more lived-in.

Mark escorted me to the backyard, which did have a grass lawn. Rob had already arrived. Knowing what Mark and I had planned, seeing a round and sleepy Rob did nothing more than bring a simple smile to my face. We said hello to each other. Nothing could stop the momentum I had now. I was doing something more than writing in a journal. And I knew I wasn't alone. Mark wasn't cursed.

Mark set up a tripod and the camera, while Rob gathered some firewood for my burning. I approached Mark. "Do you know how this thing works?"

"Of course."

"I mean more than just pushing record."

He wasn't impatient with me at all. "Yes, like I said I have made several shorts before."

"I mean, what about the mechanics of the video camera?"

He didn't know; something to do with light, electricity, and circuitry. I stopped; I didn't want to harass him while he got ready. Honestly, none of us had any understanding of any of those concepts either—what is *light* exactly? Where did the camera come from? How does the camera receive power? Where's the power plant and how does it work? How do viruses interact with a human body? It all seemed like magic.

Mark had to adjust the tripod more, so he handed me the video camera. How light it was! How little I understood anything about it! I aimed the camera at Rob as he gathered wood. He seemed even more uncomfortable when I hit 'record,' and the red light beamed at him. Ha, what does anyone else really know about technology in video-cameras. My father could probably use larger words and repeat vague concepts, but he certainly couldn't build one from scratch. How could we defeat an ancient witch's covenant? Yet with this weapon in my hand, I had a chance of playing a part.

I handed the camera back to Mark and went inside to change into my colonial rags. When I returned outside, I saw Rob and Mark had finished with the wood pile. They had a small platform in the center with a wooden pole sticking up the top. Mark also had a large fan to blow my hair up, as if the heat of the fire would make me a fashion model immediately before my death. Mark gave us the run-down of what he wanted to shoot. Some close ups of me before the fire with a blue sky background, my dirty feet on the platform from my point of view, me screaming, close ups of Rob and himself cheering, and, of course, my speech. We started filming, but it wasn't until the fan turned on, whirring the wind into my face that I felt excitement. I composed myself and gave my speech.

"You don't have to do this. I am not with the witch's covenant, although I have been experimenting on you, to learn about you, to infect you, to get what we need from you. I am only one of many, but burning me won't stop them. I can teach you how to defeat them."

My voice grew more urgent. I glared down at my feet as I continued, "once you are cursed we will rest in your mind, watching everything you do, but once we need to control you, we will, this is the ultimate curse." Rob angled the fan at me.

My voice had some pain in it now, "we will force you to drink more of the curse to strengthen it. They'll put this ultimate curse in your drink, it will be blue." I finished with a blood-curdling scream as I burned alive.

We had to shoot the speech three times because Mark wanted to have different camera angles. Mark was right, Rob seemed completely confused, slumbering around, his face perplexed. He stood to the side with his mouth open.

Mark taunted him, "better than cursing your balls off, huh?" Rob didn't answer. "What do you think?"

"Um, yeah, that's cool. How did you come up with that?"

I didn't want Mark to get too cocky, so I answered Rob, "it's like you said about 'liberty'; peoples' ideas change over time. We wanted to have some historical comparison, like Mr. S. said."

Rob really didn't seem to understand; perhaps the curse controlled him at this point. Sure enough, he started pestering Mark for a snack break, although I doubt Mark would be storing any Tru Blue in the house. Mark said we should finish up first.

Before I gave the speech for the last time, Mark wanted to try a camera trick where I would be safe behind the burning wood, but on camera it might appear I was in it. As they moved the platform, Rob handed me the BBQ-styled lighter. For whatever reason, I clicked the flame on and brought it to the skin on my forearm. My peach fuzz turned to a light noxious smoke and the pain stung badly. Yet there was some truth in the feeling, the stinging pain was trustworthy. It was something to count on. Suddenly I remembered the black-and-white photo of a screaming naked model in Michelle's office.

Once the boys had the fire going, I told them the pose I wanted to make as the fire consumed me, the pose of the naked model. Of course with my brown, rag-dress, I wouldn't look quite the same, but with the wind in my hair, I could do the same smiling scream.

We took another take of my smiling scream because Mark was not too sure the fire trick had worked. By the time we finished shooting, I felt a renewed sense of purpose and confidence. We had constructed our flag, now we needed to fly it, and see who would stand up with us against the witches and the curse.

"So what do we do now?"

Mark put everything away. "I'll do all the editing, so you're pretty much done." Rob was inside so I could speak openly. "And then we'll post it on YouTube, but how will we explain it to others who do not completely understand it?"

"Since I'm doing all the editing and Rob is doing the other skit for the presentation, I think you should post the YouTube video with an explanation." Rob approached us from the house. Mark was right, the video was too cryptic without the proof of Michelle confirming it, which would be a perfect way of exposing her and the curse. A witch would have more authority to prove witches existence than I ever could.

My mother arrived to pick me up and we all quickly parted. Mark reminded me of the necessity of my future task. "Don't worry if you don't have an account yet, it's really easy, and send me any other info you'd like me to put in the video." With that, I gave Mark a tight hug and thanked him. Feeling his arms hold my sides and push me back an inch, I loosened my arms' grip around his shoulders and we were face to face, close enough to feel each other's breath. The presence of my mom's car burned, and Mark must have felt it too, because instead of kissing me, he pulled me in close and finally gave me a proper firm hug.

• • •

That night I needed to accomplish a lot. Surprisingly, I found the application to automatically send a voice recording to an email account. I also opened a YouTube account and came up with a plan of how to talk with Michelle alone in person. While testing the application my grandmother called.

My grandmother had always lived far away my entire

life. For the last few years my mom has been saying "her health has been deteriorating," which is rather ominous. In our many telephone conversations I've never heard her mention going to the doctor for anything. Yet you could tell, what my mom meant by "deteriorating health." She had trouble remembering.

Our conversation was rather long ranging. She seemed lucid this time, I suppose she wasn't on any medications and was having a good day. It's easy to tell when she is doing well; she remembers that she starred in the musical *Fiddler on the Roof* in high school. When she isn't doing well she somehow recalls starring in any number of musicals or plays. Sometimes it's one of Shakespeare's, other times it's *Death of a Salesman*, which doesn't really sound like a musical. The last test was whom she played.

"Oh it was a long time ago sweetie, but I think I was Funny Girl." *Fiddler on the Roof* is not a comedy. I somehow doubted that character was in the musical. "Oh, I don't remember that character."

"She was the lead sweetie. You got to have your mom take you to see it again. One of those World Wide Web dating companies is sponsoring a production here. So how are you doing with the boys out there?"

I told her a little bit about Mark. "Why don't you tell him some of those things?"

"I can't say that Grandma."

"We used to write letters, I suppose no one does that anymore?

"Not really, it'd be weird."

"Well a letter gives you time to think, so you don't sound like you're coming on too strong, you might even be able to pull back if you'd like."

"Alright."

"Well, you'll have to show me this film you spoke about once you all are done."

I didn't tell her about my speech, but I did give her the general story: a woman is burned because a trial found her to be a witch, but she says she was "something else."

In her kind, somewhat patronizing way, she said it sounded interesting. I decided to just ask her out of the blue. "What do you think about witches Grandma?"

Grandma was either genuinely having trouble communicating, or she knew what I was onto, but couldn't be sure it was safe to speak to me. I had to ask several questions just to get her meaning. She didn't want to use the word "witches" though.

She said people seek blame. Everything has a cause, and sometimes things are hard to understand and it's not enough to go to church and pray the devil leaves. Sometimes a guilty party must be found. The interesting thing is that the accusers, the ones complaining, are often the ones to blame. Most people are *lazy*, *fearful* or both. She seemed to be making sense, yet I didn't quite understand how she felt about the witches.

I pressed her, and again she would not comment directly on witches. She continued: take the Nazis, clearly an evil government; genocide, torture experiments, concentration camps; it was all apparent to the German people. They knew some of the stuff happening. If a government sent police into ethnic neighborhoods, and smashed every single window in every single shop owned by an ethnicity, and beat up anyone who got near them, what would you think? Although many Nazis had courage, they were lazy; forming and sticking to convictions takes a lot of effort and they didn't question or try to have a better government. Many Germans, not necessarily Nazis, feared what the government would do to them, and for good reason. In fact, many of the people who resisted did die. What would you have done Eleanor?

I said I didn't know. My grandmother was certain, better to die fighting for what you believe than to cower in apathy. She admitted that she may not have ever experienced such a test of bravery before. Not too long after Germany had become one country again, my grandmother visited. So I asked her what she thought of the people now, and her tone changed.

Now the education system washes blood over the hands of the children, they are given the responsibility for their ancestors' faults, a terrible burden no children should have. And while it seems that most Germans are not lazy, they are mostly cowards, probably because most of the brave died in resisting the Nazis or in the Great War. Thankfully, enough brave and thoughtful people defeated them. I mentioned that we had gotten way off the witch burning topic at this point.

"No we haven't."

"Grandmother, where did we start?"

"When people blame others for things they cannot explain, the fault is often *their* laziness or fearfulness, at some point. Now I have to go."

I paused for an instant, "ok, do you want to talk with Mom."

"No, I have already dealt with her, but I have to go now sweetie."

"Oh, ok, love you."

"I love you too." And with that she hung up. I sat

motionless on my bed for some time after I set the phone down. I decided she could be trusted, but I couldn't be so up-front with her over the phone again. I would have to speak and think differently.

I went to the kitchen, got a knife and put it in my purse. I figured out the logistics and wrote down the bus routes and times. I drew a small map of the city area I would be in. I imaged a story for my mom. I checked my email: one from myself, the voice recording, another from Mark, the completed video of the witch burning.

My secret recording was a success, I could hear myself clearly. And Mark did an excellent job for his part too. In the video, the crowds yelling at me looked a little out of place, but he did a good job of catching my screaming pose. I uploaded it to YouTube.

My plan was simple: confront Michelle with the video and get her to talk about the curse while I secretly record her on my phone. My phone, in case I don't make it back, sends the recording of her to Mark, who adds them to the end of the video for everyone to hear. Sitting alone in my room, I called Michelle to make the appointment.

CHAPTER NINETEEN

The acceptance of my money, gaining my admission to the bus, almost felt like a crime. I certainly wasn't supposed to be on there. Humming and churning, the bus ushered me into the city. Strangers with heads fixed straight ahead silently grinded their teeth. From where I sat, I couldn't watch the approaching city. The sun had already set. The darkness outside covered anything of interest from view; I sat in silence, eyes fixed on the window, contemplating my purpose.

Approximately half way, the rain started. I had prepared for nearly everything, yet the weather slipped my mind. At least for now I was isolated from the rain, and everything else.

An elderly woman, noticing I was without an umbrella, offered the newspaper she was reading. "You don't want to get wet on a night like tonight, might get lost," her yellow teeth flashing, she presented an all-too-knowing smile. Nevertheless I held out my hand in acceptance almost as an afterthought to anything my face might have said. Right before the paper reached my hand, she jerked it back. I kept focused on her, although her only concern was the newspaper. Taking out a bone-white, cheap-plastic pen, she made a few small marks on the page and handed me the paper. She had marked an advertisement for Tru Blue: the annoyingly delightful, smiling boy in the ad now had on a pirate hat with a matching mustache, not entirely on his face though.

"You don't need any of that stuff, shouldn't want it either, too much sugar and it grows mustaches," she finished with a chuckle only an old lady could pull off. Neither of us spoke the rest of the way. Once we reached the massive buildings, the elderly woman once again flashed her yellow smile and left. I was alone.

The thought struck me—I am going to fail. Immediately, I corrected my thinking, stayed positive, and told myself to fix the problem. What to do? *I needed a mask.* The thought was so preposterous that I laughed. I looked at myself in the reflection of the window and pictured myself in a mask, a blue mask of course, with my boring brown eyes peering out. I planned on exposing— uncovering, unmasking—the Agency's plans and at the first sense of panic I think of covering my beautiful face? I smiled. I hadn't thought myself beautiful since working for the Agency.

The bus reached my stop; I took one glance at the silly drawing and couldn't help but smile again. Too bad it wasn't that easy; the curse was much more complicated. What I was doing was an absolute necessity.

Before I even stepped off the bus, I could feel the rain thundering down on the pavement. With two blocks to jog, I got wet. The extra weight of the rain was undeniable, but thanks to the newspaper, I do not believe any of the cold water ever hit my skin. I was still warm by the time I reached the building.

As soon as I entered the building, I threw away the newspaper, I had told Michelle my aunt would be taking me. In the elevator, I finally checked my watch, almost perfect timing, barely three minutes late for my meeting with Michelle. I expected some people to be there. After all, the last time I ventured into *Incantando's* offices, they were full in the late evening. This time, I was greeted by silence and darkness—no receptionist, no test subjects— just a single light. Behind the receptionist's desk, stood a closed door. I had never noticed a door there. It could only mean one thing: turn back now, not welcome, the door is closed. In fifteen minutes another bus could have took me all the way back to my suburb.

The door handle made a slight metallic click.

Once I passed the empty conference room, I knew the office had not a soul in it besides mine. Everything was still, no machinery hummed; even the few long fluorescent lights shone silent. Turning the last corner, I could see Michelle's office door open, shining a pale indigo light into the hallway.

My hearing became more acute and my eyes had long adjusted to the lower light, yet the pale indigo glow now dulled my vision and pulled me closer. The door was opened inward and away from me so that I could not simply reach around and knock. Inching closer, I simply turned and positioned my body in front of the office, silent.

Illuminated by a computer screen, Michelle's face had a deep concentration. Her hair was longer since I last saw her, and with some dark lipstick she had a more mature and sophisticated appearance. In fact, I had the sense that she had fooled me about her age before; I knew now that she was much older. I could see some lines around her mouth and eyes. The computer screen remained the only source of light in the office. Even with the window blinds open, the screen's image did not reflect off the window. Michelle's tall leather chair blocked any blue light that escaped her face. Her eyes blazed a bright indigo.

Her slim lips started moving but no words came out. A smile started in her blazing eyes, then in the corner of her moving lips and finally emerging in her brilliant teeth. She stopped mouthing the words from her screen, and her smile settled into the corners of her mouth again. Her eyes raised from the glow and gazed directly at mine. "Please come in and shut the door behind you."

She watched as I did as I was told. Michelle turned the ceiling lights onto a middle level, yet Michelle's face still had shadows from her pale indigo screen. "Your aunt is not coming too?"

"She's in the parking garage; I guess she had some stuff to do."

"Well, I'm glad you could make it. I assure you that we are taking this issue of an agency employee chasing you very seriously."

I nodded my head in agreement, although this was a surprise for me. We never spoke about why we were meeting. How could the man chasing me have gotten back to Michelle?

Michelle was unusually business-like, "please describe for me what happened." I started with soda machines during a restroom break. I had described what happened to my parents, perhaps my mom relayed the story to Michelle. When I finished describing the chase, leaving out Burger King, Michelle asked for a description of the man. I described him honestly, middle-aged, brown hair, average.

"Did he have any distinguishing characteristics?"

The words flew out of my mouth, "he was painfully average."

Michelle didn't take her eyes off me for a while. "I'm sorry to hear about what happened, that must have been frightening."

"I'm fine."

"Really? Because you seem really nervous right now. He is not here I promise you that."

I hesitated for an instant, "I want to show you something, it's a video."

"Oh?"

"I already sent you the link in your email." I would have to start the voice recorder while she was busy watching. I didn't want to appear too unnatural reaching into my breast pocket.

"Oh," Michelle focused back on her screen. "So, you say your aunt is in the garage?" "Yeah, yes."

As she typed in her password, she remained staring at the screen, "Hmm, did you just want to check the rain outside before you came up?" I stopped reaching for my breast pocket. "Cause your shins are wet."

"Oh yeah, it's raining pretty hard."

With a click of the mouse she announced, "here you are... you must have sent it on the way over." I had my phone automatically email the link. Before Michelle leaned back into her seat she turned the speakers up. My hand reached my breast pocket and felt a small compact notepad—and no phone.

I lost my breath and started gasping. Michelle focused on the playing video. I checked both pockets for my phone, nothing. I could feel my pant pockets, they were certainly empty, but I already knew my phone was in my other jacket. How could I believe the journal notepad was a phone? My hands took the diary out.

Michelle's mouth evolved from a dimpled smile to plain indifference. As the video played her lips pierced tight. She was not happy with what she heard. My own voice sounded so distant, a little more nasal then I would like it to be, "infected we will rest in your mind, watching everything you do, but once we need to control you, we will..." How could I forget my phone? And all I brought was the little notebook diary with all my thoughts.

Finally, my own scream ended on the screen, and I knew it would be all over for me. After the video finished, Michelle immediately twisted around and looked at the black-and-white photograph of a screaming woman on her wall. Her face twisted into a nasty frown, she became more perplexed and a bit irritated. "What are you trying to say to me Eleanor?"

I couldn't answer.

"I mean, I get what you are trying to say, but why?"

I found my voice once again, "I know who you are."

For an instant, she seemed hurt and confused, or perhaps not, because her face was stern for a moment and then she went loose. She leaned back in her chair and gave me a slight smile, just enough for the dimples to show. "Eleanor, perhaps we should talk about what goes on here. I know a lot of people out there think advertising agencies are 'evil'."

"I've seen what's going on here; I've seen the experiments you run on people, the machines you use."

"Eleanor," she let out a sigh, "perhaps I should have explained more about what we do here, before you got started."

"There's no way I would ever help a witch."

Michelle smiled again, started to speak, and then stopped. Then she asked how come I had a notepad in my hand. I told her it was my journal containing what I had discovered about the Agency. She asked to read it, and before I knew it, I handed it to her. She quickly read through the few pages of journal notes, as my heart raced. Her left hand rubbed both her eyebrows hard.

"Eleanor, let me show you something."

The wind gusted outside. Droplets of rain hit the window. Michelle typed as she spoke, "I want to show you an example of the pinnacle of human existence."

She slid the flat screen-monitor so that we could both see it without moving from our seats. A video began to play.

"What you are watching is the combined effort of numerous professionals," she looked over at me to see if I understood, "people with a lot of education, PhD's."

She focused back at the screen, so I did too—a montage of images of a romantic couple having fun on a summer day. Michelle continued speaking, the video had no sound, "thousands of hours of work, not just for this video, but the whole concept for the brand. We had an anthropologist, a Jungian psychologist, a sociologist, MBA's."

I had a hard time keeping track of the video, although it

couldn't have been more than thirty seconds long.

"You might not know what exactly those professions are, but I assure you, each of them has knowledge accumulated throughout history."

The last image on the screen contained a brand of bottled water. Free rain continued to pour from the sky. Michelle became more enthusiastic.

"We also did empirical studies—MRIs, computer captured blink rates—to ensure people literarily wouldn't take their eyes off the screen. So you see, we have explored the mysterious abstract areas of the human mind, as well as the superficial reactions, which by the way, we are beginning to understand are the most important things to ensure recognition, retention and ultimately—a purchase."

"You think *that*," I gestured with my head towards her screen, "is the pinnacle of human beings?"

"Eleanor, what did you see? Purity. Redemption. Free will. All of this can be experienced now. The act of drinking this water is now linked to deep emotional and even spiritual needs. These are values everyone aspires to and now they are within reach. I mean, what is 'purity' after all? Well, now I can hand it to you in a bottle."

I would never have guessed this would happen. My video and journal notes made her say this? Michelle seemed frustrated at my lack of reply to her comments.

"You're probably wondering how you fit in with this. The truth is that all of advertising is really based on one simple idea. And you're different Eleanor, because you have balance and can find the way out of it."

Confusion is something of an understatement at this point. Finding a way out?

"People make comparisons to other people all the time,

usually people similar to themselves in some ways, like a similar profession or age or whatever. People will compare themselves to someone uglier to feel better about their own appearance. To get a better idea of where they stand and what they are capable of, people will compare themselves to someone whom they perceive as the same level as themselves. So like, Kelsey looks as good as me, and what a cute guy she is dating. Or, Bob had the same grades as me; now check out the job he landed. People will also make upward comparisons to inspire themselves. This is where ads usually come in. All the really clever ads will play on two or even all three comparisons."

"Ok, but I still don't understand what you mean by not finding a way out."

"Well, it's all relative right? Say you're from a Pacific island, right, like where everyone is heavyset. So your comparison of what is skinny and what is heavyset is different than someone in Switzerland. But you are always comparing yourself to others so you *only* understand where you are compared to other people."

"But we do know what is too fat and too skinny for people."

"Oh, so what the doctors say. What's healthy right? What is health?"

"Um, well, not being sick."

"Is that what you think the ideal weight is based on?"

"Um yeah, well, and like how long you live."

"That sounds more or less right. We should probably add to the criteria how often you show up for work and maybe some other things. But my point is who cares? I do things that I am sure lower my life expectancy and it doesn't bother me. Health is a relative concept too; fat and skinny even more so. And of course, you'd have a harder time telling me what is a normal face."

I sat on the edge of my seat, still. "Ok, so I live on some island where everyone is big, and I am less heavyset, but when I move to Europe, now I am the heavyset one, because everyone there is skinny."

"Relatively skinny."

"Right, so what do you mean by finding a way out?"

"Well, where do new ideas come from? I mean if everyone is wearing a certain kind of jeans and people are comparing their 'look' or bodies to other people wearing those jeans, how does a completely new style emerge?"

"Someone wears the new jeans."

"Who's that someone?"

"Well, models I guess."

"And that's the upward comparison—a model is what other people aspire to be like."

"But everyone else is trapped."

"Actually no, what we are learning, and why *Incantando* is so successful: is that not enough customers really look up to those models. Having something forced down people's throats doesn't always work. No, someone else actually breaks the loop of comparisons and it's not always models on a runway."

She wanted me to guess again. She looked really intently at me and gave me a wide dimpled smile. "You, Eleanor."

"What?"

"People respect and trust you, Eleanor, you must know that, we're rarely wrong here."

Previously, I had noticed and thought about this fact: most of my friends, at least at my old school, trusted my opinion on nearly everything. My friends usually start saying the same words as me. Several times I noticed my friends buying the same thing a few days after I had.

"I believe you even said that is what you wanted most during your interview. People don't really care about social *status* anymore," she seemed to find the idea distasteful, "today, people care about *admiration*."

"I still don't understand why you wanted me though."

"I'm not saying you designed the new jeans, a designer or some kid came up with the new fashion, but somehow, someway: you see it, you buy it, and you might change it a bit. Then all your girlfriends, who think of you as a slightly higher upward comparison, copy you. You're cool. You're a *spreader*."

"But I do make comparisons, I was thinking of it while you were talking and I do it all the time."

"I didn't say that you didn't. At some point, you have the confidence, independence and curiosity to try something new. The fact that you do care sometimes is important too, if you never cared what people thought then you might originate a new idea, but to spread an idea you need to make it more stylish to the taste of others."

The photograph on the wall appeared differently to me. She screamed because she was nude, and the smile was only for appearances. But in her eyes, the way she saw the world, she was truly horrified about her body, despite the fact that her body was so incredible. She screamed from an extreme discomfort caused from any interested observer and their conditional and judgmental gaze. She truly was unsure of her beauty because she allowed others to define her beauty.

Michelle was completely right.

"So that's the way out."

"Yes and very few people know the way. Ha, even that model you talked about might be stuck constantly comparing herself to other models. You know she just gets paid to walk around in the clothes; it's not like she picked them out like you did."

Michelle was as calm as the rain had become outside, a steady and earnest drizzle. She was relaxed and confident in her big leather chair; she was enjoying herself and my company. She rarely flashed her dimples; there was no show being put on here.

"The reason I am telling you all this is because I see a big difference between you and a celebrity endorsement or a fashion model walking down a catwalk. Why I love what I do has everything to do with young adults like you." A strange emphasis was put on 'you.'

"I don't force products on people. I take the information that *you* provide us with to have the companies produce what *you* want." I doubt Michelle's voice was changing, the word just sounded so differently to me. "I am empowering *you* to change the world around *you*. I understand that you have a lot of pressures: school, your parents, other authority figures, but what we do is liberate the youth, we want *you* to be yourself and think differently."

She paused. She was becoming visibly excited again. After a breath she asked, "what are you thinking?"

A pregnant silence filled the air. "Well, I guess that's cool."

"And what we do is much deeper than this." I suppose this would have been my plan coming to fruition if I only had my cell phone and of course, if Michelle was what I thought she was… Michelle continued, "we are encoding *meaning* to things. People have always wanted things throughout history: art in renaissance chapels, and gold jewelry for king and queens. People have always had status symbols and ways of showing *who* they are and where they come from. What advertising does is allow people to understand human relations through objects. Consider James Bond: he doesn't wear sunglasses and drive a car. He wears Ray-Bans and drives a Jaguar XJL, because this conveys *more* meaning."

I wasn't really familiar with the brands; I think she forgot she was talking to someone so young. Yet I still shook my head in agreement. I know that is what she wanted.

"People are happier, more beautiful, and more satisfied than ever before. And that is largely because they can afford all the products they have always wanted. And those products come with *meaning*. People want, no… need, meaning in their lives."

Perhaps she sensed that I was getting lost, but Michelle shifted and started on a new approach. Perhaps her speech was a bit over my head. My thoughts wandered to Mark's comments about pimples in the colonial era. Did people even think about pimples since no products existed?

"What about bread? I hope this isn't dating myself. It started before my time at any rate. There used to be this bread, a white bread, which claimed it had vitamins and minerals when really it was just fluff. But people loved it. The bread was already sliced, it didn't need to be broken, it was white and pure, and people thought it contained replenishment. These are values that people need to experience."

"Are you talking about Wonder Bread?"

"Ha, well I guess it still holds true until today. Here's another example, I am sure you don't just think of your clothes as pieces of cloth. Each one has a distinct personality and expresses something different. It's the same with some of the food you eat, the books you read, the bike you ride, the computer you use, if you think about it."

"I know what you mean."

"The example people use a lot is this: picture yourself working for a soap company. It doesn't matter what you do for the company, office work, factory work, driving a truck, whatever, the fact remains that soap is your life's work."

She stopped speaking, waiting for a reply, so I said, "ok."

"So what do you think, how do you feel knowing that your whole adult life you sell soap to people?"

"Um, well I guess it's a job. I think maybe that I would find something about the specific job that I'd like."

"Sure, and I am sure that you would. But how would you feel if I said your job was not about soap, but cleanliness?"

"Better."

"But it goes even further than the value of cleanliness. Soap companies have tied their individual products to all kinds of emotions: soap for womanly elegant softness; other soap for man's assured vitality; yet other soaps for childhood's innocent wonderment, and so on. So not only do people fill the need for cleanliness, both physically and as a value, but they also fill an individual emotional level that builds confidence in what you are and what you want to accomplish. Now that is something to be proud of and that is something that I do every day."

"I think I know what you mean, I can think of some shampoos and conditioners like that."

"I know people give my job a bad name sometimes. I've seen the documentaries, and the TV shows and read some of the academic literature, but they don't seem to get it. I think you might understand me now. Is there anything that still bothers you since we have had this talk?"

What could I say? What was there to say? I sat silently and answered with a quiet, "no." Michelle searched deeply into my face, "you seem disturbed still."

"Um, well it's a lot of info."

"Eleanor, Eleanor, look at me," I raised my eyes from the floor. "You don't still believe we are witches do you?" She smiled and shrugged with a look of worry in her eyes, a few wrinkles catching the light. I smiled too and let out a slight sigh, "no, no," despite the fact that she seemed to be getting older in front of my eyes.

The look of worry persisted in her weary eyes as she sat back in the chair. "You know when I first read what you wrote I was rather offended."

I forced another smile. "Yeah I could kinda tell."

"So are we ok?"

"Yeah, yeah I think so. It's just a lot to think about."

"Well if you want me to show you around some other time, I'd be more than happy to, there's no witch's cauldron-technology here, but it's still pretty cool."

"Ok."

"But now I think you should probably get home to your parents before they start to worry." She had checked the clock on her wall and I could detect some agitation in her voice.

"Ok."

Michelle got up and we walked to the lobby in silence. She brought my small journal notebook with her. We walked to the elevator; no one was around, the building still felt empty, without a soul in the place. Michelle pushed the button and started flipping through my notes on how she was a witch with the ultimate curse/virus.

Still looking at my notes, she spoke, "you probably haven't tried Tru Blue, hmm?" She finished the sentence with a dimpled smile at me. She seemed rather entertained at my blunder.

"No, I haven't."

She glanced back at my notes and started reading from them in an articulate voice, "A virus can stand-by watching..." I could hear the hum of the florescent lights, "...and let the person..." Michelle made quotation marks with one hand, "...the 'host,' continue to go about their day until the virus has a really important reason..." She stopped, thoroughly entertained at my expense, smiling at me, she quoted the rest of my sentence, "...to take control, such as drinking more Tru Blue..." the elevator binged in front of me and Michelle, with a wide grin finished, "...to refresh or become stronger."

I stood in silence and saw Michelle. She crackled aloud "ha!" and continued, "you really got paranoid for a bit there Eleanor!" The elevator opened and I walked in and pushed the "G."

Michelle faced me and opened her mouth wide in a dimpled smile and started to chuckle in silence, "Talk about a loop without a way out; you'd never know if you were cursed would *you*?" I almost moved to keep the door from shutting. "I mean, Tru Blue isn't our only client here," the doors were shutting now and Michelle's chuckles increased in sound between her words, "we handle many consumer products." Her chuckles became laughter; she looked up with an opened-mouth smile and hunched over, powering loud cackles as the doors closed.

• • •

I took a few steps back in the elevator until I bumped up against the back wall. My breathing was heavy. I panted for more and more air when it seemed the elevator contained less and less. The lights hummed and the cables buzzed loudly as the elevator sped towards the ground.

I remembered a conversation in an elevator I had with my father when I was little. I had been afraid of elevators because they might crash, so my father told me it was the safest way to travel. "Safer than roller skating?" I asked. "You might be hit by a car." Then he quickly added, "but that's very unlikely too, Elly. Don't worry so much, we'll be fine."

Nevertheless, I always could hear the buzz of the cables in an elevator. I would listen for a change in tone or pitch to at least have some warning before everyone in the elevator would come crashing down to a painful back-shattering death. People did this, for what? The memory calmed me down before I even hit the ground floor. Outside the rain had stopped and the street gleamed like it was covered in plastic wrap.

Once on the bus, my muscles finally relaxed. I had plenty to think about, yet at the very next stop, a mother and daughter entered the bus and broke my concentration.

The daughter had to be barely a year or two older than me, approaching sixteen. Considering the other people on the bus, they were well dressed and seemed to have more money. They carried shopping bags. The bus began moving before they had chosen a seat. Plenty were open, but the mother seemed determined to go further down. She was trying to get a closer look at an ad for a car, perhaps she wanted to know the price.

Something felt really pathetic about the scene, two people going out of their way for an ad. And then I saw something else, a delicate yet still profound expression of worry on the daughter's face. The mother even looked at her at that instant. She did nothing. She didn't show any sympathy, not even recognition that her daughter was vexed. Disgusted, I turned away.

Why was it Michelle, and not my mom, who was the one to calm me down and explain things? Trying to take my mind off the mother and daughter, I glanced at their ad. The purpose of the ad was obvious, to sell a car. Michelle would say the meaning or value of this particular car is—safety, mobility, and happiness, or something like that. How silly this smiling ad-woman appeared. I certainly didn't *need* a car. Should I even *want* one?

I rode the bus on a sideways seat. I didn't face forward or backward, but I could see both ways. From this vantage point, I could easily see around the entire bus, using a mirror hung in front for the driver to see back. Everyone else faced forward. I got my black pen out of my jacket pocket, and opened it. A moustache is not a good distinguishing feature.

When I sat back down, a black man's voice came to me, "hey as long as it's not on the seats." I turned back to see the speaker, "oh no, never."

He was an elderly black man dressed in a suit and holding a well-worn wooden cane. He glanced at the ad and let out an elderly chuckle, "that's," gesturing to the ad, "not what I want to experience out of life. But a clean bus, I want that."

"I know, only ads."

Once the elderly man left, I was again free to let my thoughts wander, specifically circling Michelle's loop of comparisons. She had said, "courage, independence, rebelliousness." What had I done before? Well there were those shoes, and the scarves. What had I thought: courageousness? Or did I think I was a rebel? Perhaps, when I first thought about wearing the new clothes this was the case, but when I left the house that first day—I did not care.

I simply did not care what other people thought, felt, saw, or said about me.

EPILOGUE

Mark tuned off the lawnmower and wiped his sweaty brow with his right forearm. I got up from the shade of the house and saw the pattern he had cut in the lawn. The front door of the house swung open, and a man stood in the doorway with two sweaty cans of cold sodas in his hands. "I figured you kids would be thirsty."

"Oh, could we have two glasses of water instead?"

The man appeared confused, with his head tilted to the side, yet he smiled, "ok," and went back into the house. Mark came up to me while the man was gone. "So you want to get lunch at your place now?"

"Sounds good." We both admired his work on the lawn. "I really like this pattern, random yet convincing."

"Do you want to ask the guy?" We always did this to first-time customers.

"No, you cut it. I'll do the next one." Mark and I went into business together cutting lawns. Before the second time we mowed a customer's lawn, we offered to cut any symbol they wanted. We suggested birthday-cakes for birthdays, happy faces for promotions or good grades, team logos for the end of little league seasons, etc... However, the first time we cut a lawn, we cut something that only appeared to look like a logo.

The man came back with two tall glasses of ice water. Finally he looked out at his front lawn. "Oh." We didn't charge anything extra for any lawn art, although our prices might have seemed a bit steep.

Mark acted proud of the random shape he cut into the lawn, "Pretty cool, huh?"

"Ah, yeah."

"I'll cut the rest of it for you right now, or I'll come back later."

"Ah, I think—"

Mark cut him off, "you recognize it, right?"

"What?"

Mark didn't hide his disappointment, "oh, come on..."

The man took a few steps outside into the heat. "Oh, yeah," he titled his head, tried standing on his tippy toes. "I see it now. Could you please cut it though? I don't use that telephone service. And I'm happy with the one I have now, thanks."

Mark let out some golden laughter. I couldn't suppress mine either; usually we just had a few giggles, but this guy was too much. Mark tried to stop laughing by taking another drink of water, but caught another fit and dribbled some water out on his chin. The man's expression went from confused to upset. Mark wisely gave me the glass and started the motor again.

The man sought an answer, "what's so funny?"

"Oh, it just happens all the time. People see different things in his cuts."

"Oh I'm sorry, it was a good cut. I just couldn't tell which logo it was from this angle."

My stomach tightened with laughter and my eyes started to tear as I clenched my teeth. Finally I told him, "no, just what you said after that."

"Oh, well, I am sure you'll get someone to switch over," he leaned over and patted me on the back, "keep trying."

At my house, we stopped on the walking path near the front door. "I think it's really cool." Mark started making comments about our new front-yard. Somehow I got it into mom's head that it would be cool not to have grass; instead we simply have some indigenous bushes and trees. It could have been something to do with her making the house her own though, since she divorced Dad. I knew why Mark had stopped at this point though; no one could see us from inside the house or from the driveway side of the house. Only people further down the street would be able to see us, but no one was outside.

Mark finally leaned in to kiss me and I met him halfway. His distinct taste sent a quiver throughout my whole body. While kissing him, I once opened my eyes barely enough to see him through my eyelashes, and I saw how he always looked when we kissed—his eyes were closed.

ABOUT THE AUTHOR

ND Kalna lives a minimalist lifestyle in New Orleans without a car, spouse, children, or pets—although a fishbowl might be suitable in the future.

www.ingramcontent.com/pod-product-compliance
Lightning Source LLC
Chambersburg PA
CBHW021031130626
46552CB00005B/1789